THE Boyfriend EFFECT

New York Times & USA Today Bestselling Author

KENDALL
RYAN

The Boyfriend Effect
Copyright © 2020 Kendall Ryan

Developmental Editing by
Rachel Brookes

Copy Editing by
Pam Berehulke

Proofreading by
Virginia Tesi-Carey

Cover Design and Formatting by
Uplifting Author Services

About the Book

I'm not boyfriend material.

If a trail of broken hearts and a piss-poor record of failed relationships have taught me anything, it's this. My buddies are happy to give me shit about my latest breakup from here to next Sunday. Thanks, but I'd rather have a root canal.

And a vasectomy.

At the same time.

Relief comes in an unlikely package—the gorgeous and feisty Maren. She just so happens to be my best friend's sister, so that's not awkward at all.

But I'm a man on a mission, and Maren is down to teach me all the ways I've been failing as a boyfriend. Apparently, there are many. And it's all very informative—until I start to catch feelings.

Now it's not just my reputation on the line, but my heart too.

One

HAYES

’d like to tell you I have my shit together. That I have it all figured out.

But if you saw me standing here right now, on the sidewalk in my boxer briefs—for God and everyone to see—you’d know I’m totally full of shit.

My now *ex*-girlfriend stands on the balcony of her second-floor apartment, glaring down at me, dressed only in a peach-colored silk robe. Her hair is loose and her face is red with anger, but there are no tears.

“You bastard!” Samantha cries out and throws another armful of my clothing over the balcony. One of my socks gets stuck on a tree branch.

I grab my T-shirt from the sidewalk and tug it

on. It's May, but it's still chilly in the mornings, and the cool air nips at my bare skin.

My shoes are thrown down next—one at a time. One bounces into the street, and I wait for a city bus to pass before I retrieve it.

I look back up at Samantha, bracing myself for what comes next. In her hands is my laptop bag. *Fuck.* Complete with my laptop, because I'd come here straight from work last night.

A few of the neighbors have stepped onto their balconies to see what all the noise is about. Swallowing my pride, I tip my chin at Mrs. Hendrickson from apartment 202 and smile. Her eyes widen in surprise.

"Jesus, Sam, be reasonable," I call out.

My laptop bag comes sailing over the balcony next and lands with a loud crack on the sidewalk. There goes my laptop.

I have no fucking clue where this Samantha came from. She woke me up this morning with sex—seemed like a good sign, right? We've only been dating for two months, but I thought things were going well. Turns out, I don't know shit about shit.

Maybe she wanted one last ride? Something to

remember me by?

Fuck, I was so wrong.

I scrub my hands down my face.

"You'll never commit," Samantha says, her voice trembling with rage.

That's not true. I've eaten the same brand of cereal for the past twelve years. I know a thing or two about commitment. But I decide now isn't the right time to point this out to her.

After we had sex this morning, she curled up on her pillow, gazing at me with a soft expression. "Where do you think this is going with me and you?" She touched my chest, her fingertips tracing lazy circles on my skin.

I told her the truth, that I wasn't sure but that I liked hanging out with her. Apparently, that was the wrong answer.

She sat up suddenly, tugging the sheet up with her to cover her naked chest. "That's what you think this is? *Hanging out*?"

"No, of course not," I said, instinctively back-pedaling.

"I'm almost thirty, Hayes." She squinted at me.

I'm almost thirty too, but I wasn't sure what

our ages have to do with anything.

"I want more," she said, frowning. "A relation-ship. A real commitment. Marriage. Babies. A fam-ily."

Things went south fast after that.

I've known her for two months, so I thought what we had was just casual. I haven't even intro-duced her to my grandmother yet, who lives with me. Hell, Samantha has only been inside my apart-ment once. She's never spent the night, a fact she reminds me of regularly with disdain.

Another neighbor peeks his head out of his window, a coffee mug in one hand, a yipping dog in the other.

Cars drive by, some slowing down to watch the drama unfold. I can't say I blame them. This is cer-tainly the most exciting way I've started a Friday morning in a long time.

Finally, my jeans are tossed over the balcony, and I rush to catch them. My cell phone is still in one pocket, miraculously intact. I tug on my jeans and shove my feet into the pair of Vans I rescued.

Without another word, Samantha marches in-side and slams the sliding glass door.

Mrs. Hendrickson heads back inside too.

Show's over, folks. Nothing more to see.

After snagging my laptop bag from the sidewalk, I head off down the street. I stop at the gas station on the corner and buy myself a shitty cup of coffee before I go find my car. Samantha's neighborhood is in a bustling area of Chicago. There's never any parking. But I got lucky last night, and my car's only two blocks over. Wrapping a hand around the warmth of my cup, I head in the direction of my Lexus.

Once I reach my car, I chuck the laptop bag with my busted computer into the back seat. As I pull out into traffic, my cell phone rings. I assume it's Samantha, thinking maybe she wants to continue telling me off, and I almost don't answer. But the name on the screen says WOLFIE.

I let out a silent groan and answer on speaker. "Hey, man. What's up?" I ask after downing another mouthful of the awful coffee.

"Need you to do me a favor," he says in his gruff voice. No *hello*. No *good morning*. Typical Wolfie.

But the bastard knows I'd do anything for him. Just like he would for me. Which is the reason why I let him get away with his caveman behavior.

"It's my first day off in like two years, asshole."

"I know, I know," he says with a chuckle.

I roll my eyes. "What's the favor?" It's no use arguing with him. I'm going to do whatever it is he needs me to do.

"I need you to go check on Maren."

Except for that.

Maren is Wolfie's younger sister. She graduated last year with a degree in social work. She's a good girl. Wants to help others. Make a difference in the world.

The problem is, I've never felt about Maren Cox the way I should have. I feel cagey when I'm around her, like a lion at the zoo, right before feeding time.

"You there?" Wolfie asks at my silence.

"I'm here."

He lets out a long sigh. "She's sick. Says she's staying home from work today. Swing by her apartment and check on her for me?"

I'm reminded of all of the other times Wolfie or Maren have called me like this, needing a favor—like when she locked herself out of her apartment, or when her car broke down on the side of the road, or that time her pet goldfish died and she couldn't bring herself to flush it. What a fucking hassle.

I remember her as a kid with a toothy smile and big eyes, always trailing a few steps behind us and calling out for us to wait up. Of course, Maren looks a whole lot different these days. She's twenty-five now, and she's grown into quite a woman. Every time I'm near her, I have to force my gaze away from her full breasts, her lush mouth, and those long, toned legs of hers.

I was there for her on the night of her twenty-first birthday, holding her hair back when she puked out the car window. I was there when she had her heart broken for the first time, when her fuck stick of a boyfriend dumped her after six months of dating. I pulled her to my chest with an annoyed sigh and she tearfully broke down, making me feel even worse.

But that was nothing compared to the pain I felt when I learned he'd broken up with her only *after* punching her V-card. I wanted to hunt him down and castrate him. I wanted to make him suffer. But of course I promised a heartbroken Maren I'd do no such thing. Instead, I had to watch her cry over that dick bag for weeks.

"Why can't you go?" I ask, even though I already know the answer to that question.

Wolfie lets out a sigh. "Inventory day. Caleb, Connor, and Ever have all been here since five."

I swallow, feeling shitty about it because I should be there too.

I own a toy company, Frisky Business, with my best friends. Yes, *those* kinds of toys. The very *adult* kind. Our business is my passion, but I haven't taken a day off in years. My partners insisted I do it—take a long weekend to myself. Practically forced my hand.

"There's no one I trust more," Wolfie says.

He's like family to me, and that means Maren is too. I made a vow to him, and I'd never break his trust.

They had it rough growing up. Wolfie did everything for Maren. When their dad drank away his paycheck, it was Wolfie who got a second job his senior year of high school. While the rest of us played video games and messed around on the basketball court, he was bussing tables at the diner to pay for her ballet classes and new school supplies.

"Yeah, I'll go," I say after a long pause.

As loyal as Wolfie is, he's always been a loner. The dude rarely calls or texts unless he needs something, but he'd also be the first to sign up if you asked him for a favor.

"Thanks, man. I owe you one," he says.

I grunt and end the call. Fifteen minutes later, I pull into the parking garage under my building.

My grandma and roommate, Rosie, smiles at me when I unlock the front door and enter the kitchen. "They actually talked you into it, huh?"

"What?"

"They made you take a day off."

"Oh, right." I push my hands through my hair. "Yeah, they did." I let out a humorless chuckle.

She pours a cup of coffee and hands it to me. "Thought you'd be sleeping in. You're up early."

I nod and accept the coffee mug, deciding to spare her the story of my breakup this morning. "Wolfie asked if I'd go check on Maren. I guess she's sick."

Rosie makes a contemplative noise. "You're a good friend."

"I guess."

She chuckles and pats my forearm. "I have plans with Marge later. We're going to the farmer's market."

"Be careful." My grandmother still drives, and I have mixed feelings about that.

She chuckles again. "Don't worry so much. Are you going to see that girl of yours today?"

I shake my head. "We're not seeing each other anymore."

Rosie raises one thin silver eyebrow at me. "You go through 'em fast. I sure hope you know what you're doing."

Me? Not a fucking clue.

After I finish my coffee, I feel more human. You'd think Sam dumping me in such a spectacular fashion would have thrown me off, and it has a little. But it's less about Sam and more about the fact that I'm starting to notice a pattern.

None of my relationships have lasted more than a few weeks, a few months at most. And the only common denominator is *me*. And Sam had a point—I am almost thirty, which isn't exactly old, but it's old enough.

Why can't I ever seem to make things work? The answer to that question nags at me, but I'm not ready to hear it.

Inside my bedroom, I shut the door and head into the adjoining bathroom. I crank the faucet to hot and step under the spray of water. Soaping myself up, I wash the scent of Samantha from my skin.

After I'm dressed in a clean T-shirt and another pair of jeans, I grab my keys and phone. I press a kiss to my grandma's cheek and head out.

Maren's apartment is in a neat tidy row of older homes that were turned into duplexes in the eighties. The rent is reasonable, and street parking is plentiful. I park in front of the brick building and climb out.

I knock on her door, and after a moment, it opens. Maren is dressed in a pair of yoga pants and a T-shirt, her long dark hair tied up in a messy bun. She's five foot five, but barely comes to my chin.

"Hayes." She smiles when she sees me, lifting up on her toes to hug me. Wrapping her arms around my neck, she pulls me close.

I touch the middle of her back, patting it once, and then release her, needing to put some distance between us.

If she knew all the dirty thoughts I have when she presses her soft tits to my chest like that, she wouldn't come so willingly into my arms. But Maren's always been affectionate. She's like that with everyone. I don't think she understands the meaning of personal space, so I try not to read into it.

Smiling at me, she asks, "What are you doing here?"

"Wolfie sent me. He said you're sick." But she doesn't look sick. Her cheeks are rosy and she's still smiling.

Maren's eyes widen and her cheeks flush. "Um, no. I'm not."

I shift my weight on her front porch. "He said you called into work sick today."

She meets my eyes again. They're the color of bright emeralds and golden autumn leaves with melted milk chocolate in the very center. Technically, the word is hazel, but it's much too simple a word to describe all the life and depth I see when I look into her eyes.

There are a lot of things I feel about Maren. Confusion. Misplaced lust. And irritation—because I've never felt about this girl the way I should have.

"Well, that part's true."

"Care to fill me in?"

She groans. "You might as well come inside."

I follow her into her one-bedroom apartment.

It's not fancy, but it's clean and always neat. A gray couch sits in the living room on top of a colorful rug. Plants in mismatched pots are lined on the windowsill, and her tiny kitchen is spotless.

"Coffee?" she asks.

"I'm good."

When Maren heads into the living room, I think I detect a limp, but she lowers herself to the couch before I can be sure.

I sit down beside her. "Talk to me, dove." It's a nickname I gave her ages ago because she's as beautiful and innocent as a white dove, and it stuck.

"It's totally embarrassing." She frowns, pulling her plump lower lip between her teeth.

Her mouth is literally perfect. I want to kiss it. And then fuck it.

See my problem?

If Wolfie knew the thoughts I have about his sister, he'd cut off my balls and shove them down my throat. And I'd deserve every second of it. Everyone knows that sisters are off-limits, and we live by a strict bro code. We have to—we're not only friends, we're best friends, and we run a business together. Keeping things appropriate and PG are my only options.

I smirk. "You want to hear embarrassing? I'll tell you about my morning and why I was nearly naked on Halsted Street, if you tell me yours."

Her eyes widen. "What the hell," she says with a laugh.

"Want me to go first?"

She nods.

I tell her about how Samantha pushed me from her bed, then banished me from her apartment when I was only in my boxers. I tell her about the neighbors who watched from their windows. The kids in their pajamas pointing and laughing.

But if I was expecting any sympathy from Maren, that's the last thing I get.

She chuckles into her fist, her eyes dancing on mine. "I swear, Hayes, you have the worst luck with women I've ever seen."

You can say that again. "Believe me, I know."

She shakes her head. "One of these days, I'm going to take you under my wing and teach you how to be a proper boyfriend."

A deep laugh falls from my lips. "Any place, anytime. But first, why don't you tell me why you're skipping work today and lying to your brother?"

Her gaze drops to the floor. "I had a little accident."

My heart thuds once. "A car accident?"

Still avoiding my eyes, she shakes her head. "A *waxing* accident."

Narrowing my eyes, I say, "A *what* now?"

She lets out a nervous laugh, and her pretty cheeks blush again. She touches one with her hand. "I wanted to save some money. So instead of going to the waxing salon like I usually do for my bikini wax . . . I bought one of those at-home kits. But I think the wax was too hot."

Fuck. Me. If I thought my morning started out rough, it's nothing compared to the agony of having to sit here and face this gorgeous girl telling me she burned her pussy with hot wax.

"Shit. Are you okay?" I ask, barely managing to get the words out.

She chews on her lush lower lip. "I'll be fine. I'm just a little sore. And don't you dare breathe a word of this to my brother."

I hold up both hands. "Believe me, I don't go around talking about your vagina with your brother, and I have no plans on starting anytime soon."

This gets a grin out of Maren. "It's mortifying enough that you know."

I nod in agreement. Because now I'm picturing Maren's smooth, bare pussy, and definitely feeling a little homicidal over the idea that she did this for some undeserving guy.

"You don't have to be embarrassed around me," I say, opening up my arms to her. "Come here."

Maren moves nearer on the couch, sighing as she leans in close enough to rest her head on my chest. My heart thumps out an uneven rhythm as her scent—vanilla and fragrant shampoo—surrounds me.

Her trust in me is like a silent punishment, something I have to endure, because being near Maren isn't easy for me. A thousand pornographic thoughts I won't let myself entertain come at me from every angle. Shutting them down is like a full-time job, one I'm very good at.

When I release Maren from the hug, she sits up, and I raise one eyebrow.

"Want me to take a look?" I ask, mostly kidding.

"Are you insane?" She gapes at me. "No!"

I shrug. "Trust me, this isn't easy for me either. I just . . . what if you have third-degree burns or something. You might need medical treatment."

Her gaze darts away from mine again. "It's not that bad. Just a little pink. And tender."

I lick my lips. Hearing Maren use words like *pink* and *tender* to describe her pussy is actual torture.

Want me to kiss it and make it better?

I clench my jaw and fight for control. Years of pent-up sexual frustration churn in my gut.

"You want to talk about your latest breakup?" she asks, probably desperate to change the subject, and I know I am. "About . . . Samantha?" Maren says the name like a question, like she isn't sure of herself.

I sigh and lean back on her couch. "Not really. What's the point?"

She shakes her head and lets out a small sigh. "You go through women faster than I go through underwear."

I lick my lips. "Well, not anymore I don't. I'm done."

She gives me a dubious look, like she can't

quite believe the words coming out of my mouth. To my group of friends, I have a reputation as a Casanova. Not a player, exactly, more of a serial monogamist, bouncing from one girl to the next. But that needs to change.

"I need a break. No more relationships. No more women."

As I say the words, I know they're true. I do need a break from women. If I can't focus on a relationship, I shouldn't be dating anyone. It's as simple as that.

Maren's posture straightens as though I have her full attention. "For how long?"

"As long as it takes."

Two

MAREN

've never felt about Hayes Ellison the way I should have. Maybe it's because I've had a front-row seat to his revolving bedroom door.

That's not to say he's a manwhore, more like a serial monogamist, constantly dating someone new. Hayes is a romantic at heart, falling hard and fast, but most of his relationships seem to fizzle out after just a couple of weeks.

In the last few months alone, there was the massage therapist he started dating and loaned several thousand dollars to start her own practice. Then she dumped him. Then there was the wannabe chef he helped get into culinary school, only for her to break up with him once the semester started. It's always been this way. I have no idea what happened with Samantha.

But even with all the confusing emotions I've endured, there's one thing I always knew.

Hayes Ellison will never be mine.

My attraction to him is almost suffocating. To say we have a complicated relationship would be an understatement. When he's near, I burn hotter than the sun. His big, broad body seems to suck up all the oxygen in the room until I'm dizzy and almost breathless.

And now he's here, sitting on my couch, telling me he's swearing off women, and looking at me with pity over my poor, damaged hoo-ha.

"Have you had breakfast yet?" he asks.

I shake my head. It's nine in the morning. I made coffee but I haven't gotten around to breakfast yet.

"Let's go out and get something. Then I can tell Wolfie I fed you."

I nod, feeling slightly ashamed. I've lived with the idea that Hayes is only nice to me to appease my brother, and only takes care of me out of familial responsibility. There's no one I trust more, but Hayes isn't an easy man to be around. He can be demanding and intimidating.

But when he looks at me, there's a softness

in his eyes. He's always been that way with me. I'm his one soft spot, I guess. Like all the times I sought solace in his arms—when my high school boyfriend broke my heart, when my father died . . .

I shove those thoughts away because now isn't the time to take that trip down memory lane. "Can I shower first? I'll be quick."

His square jaw clenches. Apparently, I exhaust him. Like a small child. "Sure," he says finally.

And I do. With my hair up in a bun, I take the world's fastest shower. The warm water stings the raw skin between my legs, but it's nothing compared to the agony of having to tell Hayes about my injury.

Why did I tell him the truth? I could have easily made up some bullshit about pulling my hip flexor doing yoga. But instead, I came clean. One look into those whiskey-sweet eyes, and I'm suddenly confessing my darkest secrets. A tingling sensation twists through my lower belly.

Well. Not *every* secret.

If Hayes knew how attracted I am to him, it would go one of two ways. He would either laugh at me until he was red in the face, or he'd feel super uncomfortable and then avoid me for the rest of time. Both options sound like hell to me.

I sigh, scrubbing my skin a little harder than usual. But no matter how hard I scrub, I'll never wash myself clean of my thoughts of Hayes. I've spent hours fantasizing about kissing that sensual smirk off his face, wrapping my arms around his broad shoulders, pushing my hips against his rock-hard . . .

Okay, whoa. The more I let myself fall down this rabbit hole, the more maddening the pulsing heat between my heart and my core grows. My fingers run absently over my slick, tender skin.

Would it be incredibly sinful to masturbate in the shower with Hayes less than ten feet away from me, separated only by a thin door?

I push the thought away, dipping my face under the sudden blast of cold water coming from the showerhead and reaching for the knob. There's always a brutal rush of cold water right at the end. I usually get out of the tub before turning off the stream, but this morning, I need the wake-up call, and to cool down my now overheated body.

With Hayes waiting, I finish getting ready in a flash. I pull on a T-shirt and a pair of leggings from the drawer, once again mentally kicking myself for skipping laundry day this week. Work has been somewhat stressful. I look at the row of polo shirts hanging in my closet, each with the embroidered

Riverside logo, and a lump forms in my throat. Whenever I think about what's happening to Riverside, Chicago's oldest retirement home on the north side, all I want to do is curl up in bed under ten blankets, watch my favorite movies, and cry.

I don't have time for this.

Precious moments wasted, I scramble to make myself look presentable. After a dozen swipes of mascara, a few corrective lines to my eyebrows, and a vigorous finger-combing of my tangled hair—now I'm ready to go. I reach for the doorknob, already preparing my apology to the patiently waiting Hayes.

And I stop short. *Deodorant!*

I swipe the stick under my arms aggressively, shaking my head at my own reflection. Twenty-five years old, and I still don't have my morning routine down pat. Hayes's presence this morning has turned me into a frazzled mess. I really wish Wolfie wouldn't intervene so much in my life.

When I emerge from the bathroom, less than twenty minutes after I bolted inside, Hayes is still on the couch. But instead of looking at me with those big, warm eyes, he's dozed off, his long lashes casting shadows across his cheekbones.

I tiptoe toward him, debating between each

step which kind of little sister I'm going to be. Sweet and loving? Or an annoying pest? A thought as clear as Chicago's summer sky warms me with both excitement and shame.

I don't want to be Hayes's little sister.

Gently, I brush his jawline with the back of my fingers. "Hey, sleepyhead."

His eyes shoot open, blazing. His hand rockets up to mine in a shocking grasp, squeezing.

"Don't do that." His eyes burn with something intense, his pupils smoldering like honey dipped in molten lava.

"Sorry," I whisper, my eyebrows furrowed in confusion at his reaction.

His gaze travels slowly down my body, like he's taking his time before settling on my face once again. His expression is bored, disinterested, as he says, "You know better than to wake a hungry man."

And then his expression changes. There's that infuriating smirk, stretching soft smile lines from his plump lips and his impossible-to-read eyes.

It's my turn to blink. I can't look at him for too long before I run the risk of doing something incredibly stupid like kissing him.

"Being hangry is no excuse for being mean." I pout my lower lip, flexing my hand as if it's been injured.

No, he didn't hurt me. But that doesn't mean I won't let him think he did. I look down to the floor, and back up at him through my mascara. I'm an expert eyelash batter. It's the first thing you learn when your brother has hot friends.

But Hayes is immune to me. He's already standing, fishing in his pockets for his wallet and keys. Eliciting a response from this emotional see-saw of a man only ever gets me knocked on my butt. And my ego has been bruised enough by him over the years.

"Ready?" he asks.

I give him a weak smile. "Yep."

"After you, dove." Hayes flashes me a grin, and we head out together.

My brain is a traitorous bitch. Things I shouldn't let myself imagine pop into my head without my permission, and usually at the worst moment imaginable.

When he opens the door for me to the corner diner, I find myself visualizing his big body moving on top of mine. When he takes his first precious sip of steaming coffee, I feel his hot mouth pressed to my throat. When he reads his favorite menu items to me from the laminated tri-fold menu, I hear the dirty words falling from his lush lips as his fingers work between my thighs. All that sleek, male muscle claiming me, owning me, using me . . .

"Maren?"

I realize with a jolt that Hayes is waiting for me to respond to something he just said.

"I'm sorry. What did you say?" My gaze meets his, and *whoa*, Hayes looks ticked off. If I didn't know him so well, I'd be seriously concerned.

"Savory or sweet?"

Sweet. Always sweet.

"Sweet, I guess." I shrug, dropping another sugar cube into my coffee.

The tension etched in his clenched jaw relaxes as his expression eases into a smirk. How he goes from zero to sixty, and back again to zero, will always remain a mystery to me.

"You haven't changed a bit since you were eight, have you?" He sighs, leaning across the table. Even just a few inches of space eliminated between us feels like the weather in this dingy little diner has shifted. Tropically.

With flaming cheeks, I roll my eyes. "Whatever, Hayes."

I both love and hate when he brings up our history. Love, because it makes me so happy that we know each other's personalities probably better than anyone else ever could. Hate, because I'm selfish. I want the chance to make a new first impression. Too often, I wonder if I'd turn his head while walking down the street, if he didn't already see me as his best friend's little sister.

What would our first date look like?

"Just because you're hangry doesn't mean you get to be mean," he says with mock offense.

Taking in his wide eyes, downturned lips, and hand placed over his heart, I can't help but laugh. I quickly lift my coffee mug to my mouth to hide my rogue lips from smiling.

"Very funny," I whisper, rolling my eyes for the umpteenth time today. We've been together for what, an hour? I don't think either of us have gotten a word in edgewise without teasing.

If he really liked me, he wouldn't make fun of me so much.

That's in direct contradiction with one of my dad's favorite "no boys allowed" lectures. *When boys tease you, that means they like you, Maren.* But I shut his voice out of my head with a scalding sip of coffee. That's only my subconscious, trying to salvage a crush that's two decades stale. *No, Dad. When a boy teases you, he's just teasing you.*

When a server appears, we place our orders. I ask for my usual French toast with a side of fruit, and Hayes settles for scrambled egg whites with spinach. We're creatures of habit, so when Hayes asks for a side of pancakes, my eyebrows shoot up in disbelief.

"I've had a rough morning, okay? First, I practically got thrown out of a window. Then I discover that you're deathly ill." When I scoff, he levels me with a pleading glare. "I deserve this. Okay?"

His tone is stern, begging me to disagree with him. Not that I would. Eating a carb once in a while won't kill him, despite what he might think.

"I don't think I've seen you eat pancakes in a decade."

Hayes is pretty vigilant about his physique, which shows to an annoying degree. Meanwhile, I could probably find room in my bottomless belly for both of our meals. Especially if I could lick the syrup off of his—

"Maybe you don't know me as well as you

think you do," Hayes mumbles into his coffee, his eyebrows waggling. He's trying to be silly, but it's undeniably sexy.

I cross my legs, self-conscious about the ache between my thighs. "Can we not do this for like five minutes?" I huff, crossing my arms over my chest.

Hayes lifts an eyebrow. "Do what?"

"Play games. Tease, make fun, et cetera." I'm the one mumbling now. I'm known to start a fight and then wave the white flag of surrender within the first round. I've always been a peacemaker. It's just my personality. "Can we just be nice to each other?"

"Okay, we can do that. We can be nice." Hayes sits up straighter and whips his cloth napkin off the table, the silverware inside clattering everywhere, just to tuck it into his shirt collar.

I snort with laughter, covering my face and praying that no one in this diner is staring.

He waves my napkin in front of my face. I snatch it with a giggle, tucking it into the neckline of my polo.

"Tell me, Miss Maren, how are you on this fine morning?"

"Is this supposed to make us feel proper? Because I just feel dumb."

"You've never looked better. How's work?"

I don't have time to react to his compliment. My smile falls into a solemn frown. "It's okay."

"It doesn't . . . look okay." Whether he means to or not, Hayes matches my frown, his forehead furrowed with deep lines of concern. He pulls the napkin from his collar, then reaches to pull mine out too. Suddenly, the joke is over. "What's wrong, dove? Talk to me."

I sigh. I haven't told anyone about this yet. I guess it's fitting it should be Hayes. How can I say no to those honey-colored eyes?

"There was a meeting at Riverside yesterday morning. I guess one of the big donors we usually count on to make a yearly contribution decided to give it to the art museum instead. Which is, like, *great* for the art museum. They need money too. But . . ."

"Is Riverside going to be okay?" he asks, knowing how important it is to me.

I shrug, blinking back tears. "I don't know. The meeting was so serious. Usually, Peggy brings coffee cake or something, but yesterday . . . she was wrecked. I could tell she'd been up all night, crying. They outright told us to start looking for other jobs."

"Wow."

"Yeah." Now there's snot dripping from my nose, so I wipe it away with the cloth napkin.

Hayes reaches across the table, almost as if he's going to take my hand. But his fingers halt inches from mine. Close, but not close enough.

Sadness stews deep inside me, ready to bulldoze right through me again.

In that moment, our server reappears with plates of steaming food that make my mouth water. I wipe my tears away with a sheepish smile, accepting my plate. It smells delicious, and as I inhale, my sadness fades.

"Note to self. If Maren is sad, bring her sweet things," Hayes says with a chuckle.

I don't even care that he's making fun of me again, because these pancakes are amazing. And as concerned as I am about Riverside, I know worrying right now won't solve anything.

But that place is so much more than just a job to me. It's almost like a second home. And I do it all, whatever needs to be done . . . answer phones, return emails, follow up on insurance claims, the list goes on. But my favorite thing to do is to talk with the residents. Find out their stories.

"Hey," Hayes says, pulling my attention from my plate until I refocus on the man across from me, whose expression is strange. Beneath the concern, there's something like . . . determination? "We're going to figure this out. I'll help you save Riverside."

I blink back my surprise. "Are you actually going to help me?"

"I said I would. What's that supposed to mean?"

"This isn't going to be like that time you ditched me at the movies to go get some with Missy Carter?" I smirk at him.

"Okay, I did ditch you, but back then, seventeen-year-old me wanted his dick sucked by Missy more than I wanted to live through senior year. I did go back and get you when the movie ended," he adds with a smile.

Reaching across the table, I swat him with the back of my hand. "Jerk," I mutter, but I'm grinning back at him.

This time when Hayes reaches across the table, our hands clasp and my heart skips a beat.

"I promise I'll help," he murmurs, his eyes locking with mine. "Whatever I can do and however I can help, I'll do it for you . . . for Riverside. You have my word, dove."

My heart goes *splat*.

Three

HAYES

Dinner out with the guys is a casual affair, and usually one I look forward to. But something feels off about tonight.

To be honest, I don't want to be here. My guess is it's because I haven't been able to get Maren off my mind, but it could also be because my so-called friends forced me into taking some time off last week, and I'm still feeling guilty about it.

Cheeseburgers and beers from McGil's solve most problems, though, so things are beginning to look up. Our server delivers our food, along with a stack of extra napkins we didn't ask for but are certain to need.

After setting down the plates, she lingers at our table a moment too long. I'm sure she sees three successful, attractive bachelors when she looks at us, and she's not wrong. But guys' night is sacred, and even Connor knows better than to go hunting for pussy during guys' night at McGil's.

"We're all set, thanks," Wolfie tells her, flashing an annoyed glance her way, and she scurries off.

Connor shakes his head at him. "She seems nice."

I watch their interaction with a distant sort of detachment, knowing I need to snap out of whatever this is. I'm distracted and edgy, and it's only a matter of time until Wolfie notices. The dude picks up on everything, and it's almost impossible to hide something from him.

"You good?" Wolfie asks, appraising me from across the table with a creased brow.

"Yeah."

"Come on, Hayes. We know you better than that. What's going on with you?" Wolfie levels me with a serious glare.

Knowing better than to blow him off, I rub a hand over the stubble on my jaw and decide to go with the answer that doesn't reveal that I've been thinking about what his sister would look like naked. "Um, shit went sideways last week with Samantha. It's not a big deal."

"Samantha? She was your flavor of the month, right?" Connor chuckles into his beer. "What the hell happened this time?"

I groan out a sound that my friends interpret correctly.

"That bad, huh?" Connor gives me a mocking look.

I grab a couple of napkins and dig into my meal. I've had longer relationships with one of these burgers than he's had with a woman. The dude's allergic to monogamy. A total playboy. He and I don't see eye to eye on a lot of things, but he's been a friend since college and is one of my business partners, so I do my best to play nice.

Because Connor's a perpetual bachelor, I don't expect him to understand my need for companionship. But I've always been this way; it's just how I'm wired. I feel more like myself when I'm part of a duo. But I must be doing something wrong, must be the world's worst boyfriend to always end up in this same position after a few weeks or months.

Wolfie glares at me. "Tell us, Hayes."

God, would it kill the guy to smile every once in a while?

"She wanted commitment, and I wasn't ready," I say around a bite of my burger.

Connor smirks. "So the usual then."

"Fuck off." I grin at him and toss a fry at his face.

Wolfie shakes his head. "Behave, children."

If I'm the Casanova of the group, constantly searching for my other half, and Connor's known for his revolving bedroom door, Wolfie's kind of like the dad of our crew. With his stern reputation and that perpetual scowl on his face, I'd say that solidifies it. I constantly feel like I'm disappointing him and can never say no, which is one of the reasons I'm always checking in on his sister when he asks. It's the least I can do. Especially because I know how much shit he and Maren went through growing up.

"Knowing you, you've probably already moved on to the next unfortunate soul," Connor adds before shoving two fries into his mouth.

I give my head a firm shake. "Nope. Not this time. I need a break, man. I'm giving up dating."

Wolfie meets my eyes and nods. "That's probably wise."

I nod back, but my feelings about this topic are

anything but settled. Part of me worries I won't be able to do it. Another part is worried I'll never find a good woman to settle down with. And still another part of me wonders why my relationships never seem to work out.

The conversation moves on to business, which is no surprise, and I find myself nodding and grunting at the appropriate times. I offer my opinion when needed or asked for, but my mind wanders.

More specifically, it wanders straight to Maren.

When she opened up during our breakfast together about her struggles at work, the somber look on her face gutted me. She has the weight of the world on her shoulders, and there's no way I couldn't offer to help. Riverside is more than just a job to her—it's the safe place she went after school. It's where she spent her afternoons visiting with her grandfather before he passed. It's part of what makes her Maren.

No longer hungry, I push my half-empty plate away. A quick glance at Wolfie confirms that he can't read my thoughts, and thank God for that, because they're not always so pure when it comes to his little sister.

As much as I try to keep myself from thinking about Maren as anything other than Wolfie's sister, it's not easy, and it's getting harder the more one-on-one time I spend with her. I want to help her keep her job, but it's not just that. I want to do a lot of things with her, if I'm being honest—both platonic and not so platonic. But if I'm going to stay single for a while, I need to ignore all those thoughts, and I might as well use my new free time for something good.

And that's when it hits me. I may have just thought of the perfect solution to help Maren. And if it also involves spending a lot of extra time with her, so be it.

Maybe it will put an end to this weird funk I've found myself in, as long as I keep myself in check and the end goal in mind.

Four

MAREN

"Hi, Maren!" Mrs. Jones calls from her wheelchair in the hallway.

I poke my head out of my office to wave hello. Her CNA, a nursing assistant, waits patiently for the exchange to be over and done with, wrapping her manicured fingers loosely around the wheelchair handles.

Mrs. Jones is a resident who needs constant supervision and care. Ever since she slipped in the tub last spring, she's been rolling on four wheels. If you ask me, I think she likes the chauffeur service.

"Hello, Mrs. Jones. How's your back feeling today?"

"Better." She smiles, the wrinkles deepening around her big brown eyes. "That massage man you brought in was wonderful. I didn't know men did that kind of work."

I smile through the cringe. It's bizarre to me what some of these older folks latch onto from their pasts . . . especially the outdated prejudices that seem to lead to these little offhand comments. But then I remember that I might not see Mrs. Jones again after this month. If Riverside tanks, I might not see any of my residents again. And I know I'd miss these conversations terribly.

"People are doing all sorts of work these days. Look at me," I say with a shrug.

"Time for breakfast and book club," the CNA says gently.

I give Mrs. Jones a nod. "I should borrow that massage therapist from you next time," I call as the CNA steers her away. "Don't wear him out, okay?"

I can still hear Mrs. Jones laughing when the elevator doors close behind them.

My stomach grumbles. I usually eat breakfast before I come to work, but ever since the staff meeting, I've had a hard time getting out of bed in time for work, let alone eating.

After finishing an email, I pocket my Riverside ID and lock my office door behind me, starting the short trek down the hall to the elevator. When it takes me to the fourth floor, Mrs. Jones and her book club are already getting situated in the restaurant with bowls of fresh fruit and oatmeal.

I pick up a tray and opt for a breakfast sandwich. The cashier nods when I flash my ID at her, pressing the buttons that put the meal on my tab—fancy words for docking my paycheck by a few dollars. The food here is surprisingly good, so I don't mind one bit.

During mealtimes, I make it a point to sit with the residents. Part of my job is to be the point of contact between a resident and their medical team. I have bimonthly meetings with each resident, as the schedule allows. Chats over coffee and cookies are just an easy way to circumvent the red tape and keep my finger on the literal pulse of Riverside.

The morning sun streams pleasantly through the tall windows that face the inner courtyard, luring me across the floor. There, I find one of my favorite people, Donald, relaxing in an orange armchair. His eyes are closed, his chest rising and falling as he dozes peacefully.

I set my tray on the coffee table as quietly as I can. Lifting my sausage-and-egg breakfast sandwich to my lips, I take a cautious bite. The crunch is loud enough to wake the dead.

"And this is the lullaby I deserve?" Donald grumbles as he cracks open his eyes, the perfect picture of a crotchety old man.

But I know he's not actually grumpy. There's always a sparkle in his stormy blue eyes, promising good humor and endless banter. I could use a little entertainment today.

"Sorry, Don." I chuckle, covering my mouthful with one hand. "The bread is toasted."

"Toasted? From that crunching, I would have guessed it's made of gravel."

"I sure hope not." I feign concern, inspecting the sandwich.

"You're new here, kid. You'll get used to it," he tells me with a wink.

We share the same smile that we always do whenever he brings up how *new* I am. To Don, a couple of years here means I'm still new. But I don't feel new. Either way, I don't mind the teasing, and I sure don't mind being called *kid* when it's Don doing it. I guess, out of all the residents here, he reminds me of my grandpa the most.

"How are you holding up today, Don?"

"Oh, the obligatory question," he says, straightening his posture like the good student I'm sure he was. "Fine. Very fine. And how are you?"

"Oh, I'm good." I smile unconvincingly, and he raises a wiry white eyebrow.

"Don't lie to me," he says, a stern edge to his voice.

Once upon a time, Don was a college professor, and a strict one at that, I've been told. There's no use hiding anything from the man. But we technically haven't gotten the green light to talk to residents about Riverside's financial woes, so I'll have to beat around the bush.

"I'm just tired. Spent the last few nights up late, trying to figure out a predicament."

There. It's true, but vague enough that it shouldn't raise any red flags. Don is skeptical, however, squinting at me like he's trying to read my mind.

Not a chance, Don.

Eventually, he relents, leaning forward with a huff and reaching out one hand. I take his palm in mine, soft and scratchy at the same time, his papery skin marked with age spots. My heart hurts whenever I remember just how old he is. Ninety-four on his last birthday. I can't handle much more loss in my life, but I also know he won't be around forever.

"I've been alive for over ninety years, Maren. And I haven't seen many people work as hard and as long as you do. If you work for it, it'll happen." With that, he pats my hand lightly and leans back into the armchair with a sigh. "Now, eat your breakfast so you can get back to it."

My eyes prick with tears, but I blink them away. I haven't cried in front of a resident yet, and I don't plan on crossing that line today.

"Yes, sir," I whisper with a wry smile.

Without another word, I finish my breakfast while Don resumes his morning nap. On the way back to my office, I flag down a CNA and ask him to check on Don in an hour. His neck cramps up if he sleeps on it wrong, after all.

Back at my office, Peggy is waiting at the door.

"I'm sorry, did I forget a meeting?" I ask, reflexively reaching for my phone to check my calendar app.

"No, no, not at all. Just wondering if we could chat for a second," she says, sounding worried.

"Of course."

Peggy follows me inside, closing the door behind her before slumping into the chair across from my desk with a heavy sigh. The moment we make eye contact, she bursts into tears.

I spring into action, grabbing the tissues from on top of my filing cabinet and sliding them across the desk toward her. She takes a tissue with a soft thank-you and wipes the tears from her flushed cheeks. The bulky beads on her necklace clatter with each shuddering breath.

"What's going on?" I ask, a lump forming in my throat as I prepare for the very worst she could say.

"Oh, you know," she says with a sniffle. "Accounts payable says we've got until the end of the month before we have to cut payroll. I'll be forced to lay off so many employees," she says, then dissolves into another puddle of tears.

It takes every ounce of stone-cold professionalism in me not to give in to the tragedy of it all and cry with her.

"Isn't there anything we can do?" I ask, my throat tight. "There's got to be something."

"Well, not that I've found. We can look into loans, but I don't know how we'd ever pay them off. Unless a big donor sweeps in and saves the day, Riverside as we know it is done for. It's just gotten too expensive to operate," Peggy chokes out.

Pulling herself together, she scoots forward in the chair, a new determination in her eyes. "Maren, you're such a wonderful, hardworking young woman. You should look for another job sooner rather than later, before everyone else starts looking. Put me down as your reference. I'll tell any potential employers how incredible you are. You would be a godsend to any employer."

"Thanks, Peggy," I say with a weak smile, wishing this conversation were over. Actually, I wish this conversation was one I never had to have. All I want to do is run out of here, hop on the Red Line, and take it straight to my uptown apartment where I can cry in peace, away from everyone.

Peggy pulls me in close and gives me a big hug before she leaves.

I squeeze her tight, knowing that whatever I'm feeling must be amplified tenfold for her. She's been here for over a decade, so I can't imagine what this must be doing to her.

The rest of my morning passes in a blur of appointments and reports. I'm pulled away from scanning my emails only by my phone dinging with a reminder.

Lunch with Scarlett.

Still numb, I pack up my purse and lock my office, stepping out into the midday glow of summer in Chicago. The café we picked is only a short walk away, and I'm reaching for the door just as Scarlett approaches.

"Hey!" she calls out, all sunshine and warmth in her flowy pink top and cream cardigan, her rainbow-hued crocheted purse slung over one shoulder.

All it takes is one look at my best friend, and the emotions of the day come barreling forward, releasing the tears I've been holding in all day.

Scarlett rushes toward me with open arms and a worried expression. "Oh my God, Mare. Are you okay?"

"Not really," I manage to say, sniffing loudly and wiping away tears that now freely stream down my cheeks.

"Let's grab a table, and you can tell me all about it, okay?"

Scarlett does all the talking, thank God. She orders my favorite soup-and-salad combo for me and a chicken salad sandwich for herself, before guiding me to the most secluded corner table available on the patio. By the time the food is served, I've tearfully confided in her about the whole depressing situation at Riverside.

"That's heartbreaking." Scarlett sighs, leaning over to rub my back with small, comforting circles. "I'm so sorry, Mare. What a disaster."

"Thanks for listening." I sniffle, dabbing at my eyes with a paper napkin. "Can we talk about *anything* else now? Please?" I blow the steam off of a spoonful of lemon rice soup.

"You know I'm always here for a good distraction. You won't believe the date I had last night. The bastard showed up in a Hawaiian shirt—short sleeves, flower pattern, garish colors, the whole nine yards."

"Nooo." I laugh, shaking my head in gleeful commiseration.

Scarlett goes on a lot of dates, and they're usually pretty terrible across the board. In her search for Mr. Right, she's compiled an extensive canon of disaster stories, all told with an incredible sense of humor. While I do feel for her latest dating disaster, I'm already perking up at the hilarious situation she has once again found herself in. She was right—she always provides a great distraction.

"Like, I know it's summer and all, but I thought

we collectively burned all Hawaiian shirts back in the early 2000s? As a society? Like, no, dude! There are rules!"

I'm full-on belly-laughing now, the drama of the day nearly forgotten. I can always count on Scarlett to lift my spirits.

When we finish our lunches and say our good-byes, I hug her a little longer than usual.

The rest of the afternoon passes by in a fog. My resident meetings are uneventful, and my paper-work even more so.

By the time I pack up and leave for the day, my mood has sunk again. The hot summer sun mocks me, still high in the sky at five p.m.

Heading for the train station, I make the quiet trek through the residential neighborhood where Riverside is comfortably nestled. I usually love this part of the day, when the work is done and the only concern on my mind is what I'll have for dinner.

Tonight, I'm numb with disappointment and helplessness. My mind is overcome with trying to figure out what I can do to help save Riverside, but so far, I've come up with nothing, which makes my mood sink even further. For once, there are no train delays, so I make it home in record time.

Parked in front of my duplex is a familiar Lexus, so I'm not terribly surprised at who I find waiting for me on my doorstep.

"Hey, dove." Hayes lounges on the steps, a lazy smile on his full lips. His shirtsleeves are rolled up, revealing intricate tattoos on his left forearm.

The sight of him sends a shiver running down my spine.

"Hey," I say softly, giving him an awkward little wave. *What is he doing here?*

"I thought we could talk options for Riverside. Are you free tonight? We could order dinner?" he asks, leaning his elbows against the top step.

I doubt he realizes it, but this posture showcases his pecs like none other. It's so unfair.

"You don't have to do that," I say, my voice coming out a little breathless.

He lifts one shoulder. "I know it's been weighing on you, and I've been thinking on it since we had breakfast last week. I think I've come up with an idea that'll work."

"Really?" I squeak, stepping around his limbs,

trying my best to ignore how close his face is to my crotch. "Come on in."

Once we're inside, Hayes settles into his usual spot on my couch, making himself right at home. It always blows my mind how shockingly natural he looks in my little apartment, almost as if he lives here too. Once again, it's time to rein in my loopy imagination of what could never be.

I kick off my shoes and join him on the couch, tucking my feet under me. "Thanks for this, Hayes. I never expected you to have any ideas."

"I'm thinking we host a fundraiser," he says, his whiskey-colored eyes flashing to mine. "Some fancy event where we can charge a couple hundred dollars per ticket. There could be a raffle and silent auctions. Prizes, auction items, and catering can be donated, the works. What do you think? Would it work?"

I can barely hear what he's saying over the hammering of my heart, but from what I gather, it actually sounds like a really good idea. "I think we could do that."

"Great. Let's write up a proposal. What do you want for dinner?" Hayes whips his phone out of his pocket, scrolling for his preferred delivery app.

I nestle against his shoulder. Maybe I'm too

physical with him, but I don't care. With such ease, he's blown in and swept the fog away. I can't help but want to touch him. Thank him. Gain comfort from him.

"Pizza sounds good," I murmur, looking down at his phone screen.

"Pizza, it is."

I watch him assemble the perfect pizza—sausage, green peppers, onions, and extra cheese. My heart flutters when I realize he's memorized my favorite pizza, and that's what he's ordering. I have to remind myself that most friends know each other's orders, and that this isn't anything to read into. Scarlett proved that today at lunch, so of course Hayes knows my pizza order.

"Okay, it should be here in a half hour. I'll get my laptop, and we can start working on a game plan." He stands and walks to the door where he left his bag to dig out his laptop.

When he comes back and sits down, there's a foot of space between us on the couch. It's a little humiliating how bummed I am, but I try not to focus on it . . . too much.

"All right," he says, "so I'll let you come up with some catchy name for the event. I can look into caterers while you make a list of potential auction items, and who we can approach for donations, yeah?"

I nod, reaching for my own laptop, which is tucked under the coffee table. I reluctantly decide to give him the space he obviously wants, curling my legs beneath me as I get situated on the carpet. Once we're both comfortable, we put our heads down and get to work. Before long, I've completely forgotten about pizza. Instead, my thoughts are wrapped up in gift baskets and experience packages.

The door buzzer scares the living crap out of me, and it feels like I jump two feet in the air. Hayes openly laughs at my shock, which only causes my cheeks to grow redder and for me to roll my eyes in his direction.

"Shut up and get the pizza," I mutter, waving him toward the door.

"Yes, ma'am," he says, standing from the couch.

Staring at his jean-clad ass certainly does nothing to calm my jitters. *How does he keep his butt so perfectly muscled?*

While Hayes moves our computers to make room for the pizza box and plates, I excuse myself to my room to change into something a little more comfortable. Closing the door behind me, I slip out of my pants and shirt so I'm standing in my underwear.

Do I have to wear a bra around Hayes? I roll my shoulders, the straps pinching uncomfortably. *Screw it, he won't even notice.* I reach around to unclasp my bra and let the straps fall from my shoulders.

When I reemerge from my room, I'm wearing a loose, striped tank top and my comfiest leggings. Hayes glances at me, but then goes back to staring blankly at the muted television screen, his brow furrowed.

"Thanks for waiting," I say, leaning over the pizza to take the first slice from the box. When I offer the next slice to Hayes, he holds out his plate without even looking at me. *Okay, then.*

"Want to watch something while we eat?" His voice is low and gravelly, and he still doesn't look at me.

"Sure."

I'm not sure how he knew that I needed this tonight. Pizza, movie, and a good friend. I'm not sure why, but that combination really makes most problems feel smaller.

He turns the volume up, settling on whatever superhero movie is playing on a loop tonight. I sink into the couch next to him, enjoying the warmth of another person so close to me. But Hayes isn't just any other person. We sit in silence through the opening credits. I take a bite of pizza, building up the courage to look at him.

Hayes is already working on his next slice of pizza by the time I sneak a glance at him.

"Do you want to stay for a while? I mean, at least until the movie is over?" I ask, barely recognizing my own voice. I sound much more sure of myself than I actually am.

That tiny, mysterious muscle in his jaw twitches. The same muscle I see jump a lot when I'm around.

"Sure, I'll stay."

Five

HAYES

This is an interesting turn of events.

My current status? I'm sitting on Maren's couch watching a movie with her. Which is fine and nothing unusual.

Except for the fact there's a fence post in my boxer briefs right now, and I can't let Maren know that. Uncomfortable, I shift my position, but it's nothing compared to the embarrassment I'd feel if she knew how hot I get for her, and the reaction my body has when she's around.

What the hell is she doing in that flimsy tank top with nothing underneath? It's taking every ounce of self-control to keep my eyes trained on the TV screen and not where they want to go.

For now, I have to focus. At least the movie is

good. And the pizza is fine, although what I want to be tasting is between her legs.

Fuck.

My focus lasted all of five seconds.

New plan.

Maybe some conversation will help take my mind off all the filthy thoughts running rampant through my brain.

"So, uh, have you seen this one before?" I jerk my chin toward the screen, where the main character is scaling the side of a building with ease.

Maren nods, her mouth full of pizza. She wipes the corner of her mouth with the back of her hand, just like I imagine she would after sucking me off.

For fuck's sake! Get it together, Hayes.

"Are you kidding? It's a classic," she says after swallowing, crossing her legs underneath her.

My brows rise with surprise. "I didn't take you for a superhero movie buff."

She shrugs. "When you grow up with Wolfie for a brother . . ."

I grunt in understanding, and a comfortable silence falls between us. The talking is helping, so I try to think of something else to say.

"So, how are you—" I say, just as she says, "I was wondering—"

Maren giggles and nods at me, but I wave her on.

"No, you go."

"I was going to ask about the caterers. Any luck?"

Right. Shop talk. The reason I'm here.

Saving her place of employment that's also very near and dear to her heart is the goal, and of course, that's where her mind's at right now. I'm the only one who can't keep his mind out of the gutter for more than two seconds.

"Yeah, I got some good leads. Here, take a look." I pull my computer from the coffee table and into my lap.

Maren climbs up onto the couch next to me and nestles into my side. Thank God for the two pounds of plastic and metal in my lap, which is all that's saving me from a world of sin right now.

We scroll through the fruits of my labor while a fight scene plays in the background. Maren makes small sounds of approval at each website, which only makes it harder to keep my cool.

"These are incredible," she says, clutching my arm tighter and pressing her cheek into my shoulder. "Thank you so much, Hayes. I don't know how I'll ever repay you."

I can think of about a million ideas . . . "Don't mention it. I'm happy to help."

I put my laptop away again—the new laptop I had to buy to replace the one Sam tossed onto the sidewalk.

The feeling of making Maren happy, of helping her when she needs it? It just might be better than sex. Not that I don't want to test that theory out before drawing any conclusions.

She lets go of my arm and throws her head back on the couch with a sigh of relief. "I feel so much better already," she says happily. "Don't get me wrong, there's plenty more to do, but it feels like things are looking up in all aspects of my life."

"Yeah? Even, uh . . ." I nod my head to her lap, and she stares back at me blankly. "You're feeling better . . . down there too?" I shift my gaze briefly to her leggings before meeting her eyes.

A pretty blush creeps over her cheeks and down her neck. She tries to suppress a smile and looks at the floor, shifting in her seat. "It's still a little tender. But yeah, it's almost all healed up."

I can still kiss it better. "Good. I was worried."

"You were worried about my . . . down there?"

Fuck, fuck, fuck. "No, I mean—in a medical sense. I just want you to be safe and healthy, dove."

"Oh. Right." Her chest stutters with an inhale.

My voice drops lower. "Burns should be taken seriously. Especially on . . . *delicate* parts of the body." *Why the hell am I still talking?*

"You didn't say anything to my brother, did you?"

"Of course not."

She sighs, blowing out a slow breath. "He'd never let me hear the end of it."

You and me both.

There's no telling exactly what Wolfie would do or how he'd react if he found out his best friend and his kid sister were talking about the state of her pussy, but something tells me he wouldn't be too stoked.

"What he doesn't know won't—"

I stop mid-sentence. Maren isn't listening to me. She's pretending to watch the movie. But really, she's curled up in a ball with her head in her hands, tears welling up in her eyes and her shoulders shaking.

"Dove, what's wrong?"

"I'm sorry. I'm just so embarrassed," she whispers. "First the waxing accident, and now Riverside. You must think I'm a mess." She swipes at the corners of her eyes, giving me a sad look that devastates me.

"Come here."

I pull her into me, looping my arm around her shoulders, and she lays her head on my chest. It breaks me to hear her talk about herself that way. Maren's the last person who should be feeling guilty about anything. And I want to make sure she knows it.

"I'm here because I want to be, okay? Not because I feel bad, and certainly not because I pity you. You're strong, smart, and beautiful. Shit happens, and we all need a little help sometimes."

"You really think I'm beautiful?" she asks, sniffling.

Fuck. This girl will be the death of me.

I smirk, trying to downplay how spectacularly I just stuck my foot in my mouth. "Don't let it go to your head."

We stay like that for the rest of the movie, Maren with her head on my chest, and me doing my best to train the crouching tiger in my pants. It didn't take long for her to stop crying and relax into me. Let's just say tonight proved she's really not big on personal space.

If Maren knew all the ways I've fantasized about taking her—pushing her hard up against a wall, bending her curvy ass over a table—she'd be horrified. She certainly wouldn't come willingly into my arms, or hang all over me like I'm her personal jungle gym.

I know a lot about women, both from my time in the dating scene and because of my job. But I don't know much about matters of the heart. The human heart confounds me. Like, how can I feel so many things for Maren, but be too chickenshit to do anything about them?

Shortly after the movie ends, I rise to my feet and Maren walks me to the door.

"Thanks for coming over tonight."

I nod, trying not to look at her chest. Yeah, lingering would only leave more time for temptation. "Of course. It's actually helping me too, you know."

"How's being here helping you?" She shoots me a questioning look.

I shift, suddenly wishing I hadn't said anything. But now that I have, I know Maren won't drop it, so I might as well be honest. "With my self-imposed break from dating, I have more free time on my hands."

Maren's expression turns thoughtful, and she nods. "We can help each other then."

"I'd like that." As the words leave my mouth, I realize they're absolutely true.

Her lips part, breaking into a happy grin. "You sure you're not going to mind when I point out all the ways you absolutely *suck* as a boyfriend?"

This pulls a laugh out of me, despite my uneasy mood. "I do not *suck* as a boyfriend."

Maren narrows her eyes. "*Hayes.*"

I chuckle. "Fine. Lay it on me."

She leans against the doorframe, appraising me with a cool expression. "First of all, contrary to popular belief, women do not like dick pics. And they show them to their friends, you know?"

Clutching my chest in mock horror, I smirk. "I'm not a total caveman. I would never."

"*Ever?*" she asks.

"My dick has never been photographed. Promise."

Maren laughs. "That's good. And you know all that stuff about women being the fairer sex is garbage, right?"

I shift my weight. "Mostly?" I say, my voice rising. "But I'm still going to open doors and pay for first dates."

She bites her lip, still watching me. "There may just be hope for you yet."

I nod, suddenly feeling unsure.

Back at my apartment, I enter to find the kitchen bright and welcoming. Leave it to Rosie to always leave a light on. I grab a glass from the shelf and fill it with water before walking to her door and giving it a soft rap.

"Oh, good. You're alive," Rosie says sarcastically.

With a chuckle, I push the door open to find her tucked into bed, curlers in her hair and a book in her lap.

"Brought you some water."

She grunts, narrowing her eyes. "Where were you out so late?"

"With Maren. She needed some help. Riverside stuff."

"It sounds like you've been spending a lot of time with Maren lately." Her eyes widen suggestively.

"I was just helping a friend. You know that."

"Mmm." She looks skeptical.

"Good night, Grandma."

"Good night, sweetheart."

I close the door to her room and walk across the apartment to mine. Once alone with my thoughts, I finally let myself breathe easy for the first time all night.

I did it. I survived. I made it one night alone with Maren without putting my hands all over her.

And it was absolute fucking torture.

Okay, this is harder than I thought it would be—the whole *look but don't touch* thing we have going on. She doesn't play fair. Maybe because this isn't really a game. It's real life. And my relationship with my best friend and business partner is on the line.

But there's more to it than that, because now Maren needs my help. We only have a month to save Riverside. I have no idea when this became important to me, but it did. I have to see Maren succeed.

Even seeing her waver for a second tonight broke me. Maybe because Riverside was the safe place she came after school to see her grandfather, back when he was still alive. Maybe because it's where she works now, and I don't want to see her laid off and suddenly thrust into the job market. But more than any of that, Maren wants this, plain and simple. So I want it for her too, and I'll do whatever I can to make it happen.

Damn, if she doesn't make all of this so complicated. Being with her tonight, just sitting there looking into her wide eyes and at her pretty little mouth was enough to drive me crazy. Add in the memory of how good she looked and felt curled next to me, and *hello, fence post, my old friend.*

I take a deep breath, fighting to get myself under control.

But then I remember her telling me about her pussy. That it's almost healed, but still tender. The innocent blush that crept over her cheeks as she spoke.

It's no use. She's ruined me.

I can't let myself commit the cardinal sin of fantasizing about my buddy's sister.

So I do what any man would do.

I squeeze my eyes shut, bite the inside of my cheek, and jack my cock alone in the darkness of my bedroom, praying that karma doesn't really exist.

Six

MAREN

For the first time all week, I can't wait to get out of bed.

After Hayes took off last night, I set my alarm early, for six a.m., so I could spend a little more time on the fundraiser before hightailing it up to Riverside. But sleeping isn't easy when all you want to do is get started on a new day. I'm already wide awake by the time my alarm clock goes off.

As soon as my feet touch the floor, my mind is brimming with event details. The timeline is limited, and we can't afford to use an event-planning service, so we'll have to be creative. Good thing I'm always up for a challenge.

Once I'm showered, I wrap myself in my favorite fluffy towel and head from the bathroom to the kitchen, leaving a speckled trail of water in my wake. The nook adjacent to my kitchen houses my laundry machines, tucked away behind unfinished bifold doors.

Popping open the lid to the dryer, I mentally pat myself on the back for having the foresight to do a load of laundry last night before I crashed. My polo is fresh and fragrant with the smell of vanilla fabric softener. Back in the bathroom, I pull my hair up into a ponytail and apply my go-to natural makeup look. I'm feeling so reenergized that I even apply a little rosy lip color to accentuate my smile.

The Wi-Fi in my apartment is uncharacteristically fussy this morning, so I pack my personal laptop into a canvas bag and move my operation two blocks east to my favorite coffee shop, Early Bird. The café is nestled between a bank and an Italian restaurant, all sharing the same building complex. Trendy little coffee joints (that aren't Starbucks) are hard to find in this neighborhood, but Early Bird beats the odds by transforming into a chic little cocktail bar called Night Owl after seven o'clock each night. I admire the versatility of small businesses, a trait I hope will rub off on me while I plan.

After I've situated myself at the window, seated with my laptop and a piping-hot latte, I get to work. By far, the process of securing auction items will be the most time-consuming, so I'm getting a head start.

When it's time for me to hop on a train up north, I've drafted over a dozen donation requests to local businesses that have supported Riverside in the past—plus a few new spots I think we'd have a shot at winning over. Restaurants, theaters, breweries, and even a bowling alley made the list.

I consider adding Hayes's company, Frisky Business, but I have a feeling a gift basket full of dildos might not go over well with this crowd. To my brother and his friends, their company is totally normal, and to me, it's no longer as shocking as it once was. But I have to remember that not everyone is as open-minded.

My ponytail swings back and forth as I confidently walk up the stairs to the train platform. The biggest challenge in all of this will be convincing Peggy, who has already resigned herself to defeat, that this will work.

"I have a contact at a liquor supplier that would definitely be interested in providing the wine for the tasting, and I have all the donation requests for the auction ready to send. My friend even drafted a design concept . . ."

I flip my laptop around on my desk and slide it toward Peggy, whose eyebrows have been deeply furrowed in confusion since I began sharing with her the plans for the fundraiser to save Riverside. She pulls her reading glasses from their home in her shirt's lapel and squints at the design.

Sometime between compiling a list of potential caterers and gorging himself on pizza, Hayes whipped together a beautiful logo for the event, using Riverside's navy-blue and gray colors with accents of silver. "Riverside Gala" practically glows from my screen, shining in the reflection of Peggy's glasses.

"What do you think?" I ask, waiting for her to say something for the first time since she sat down for this impromptu morning meeting. "Do you think the ticket price is too high? Have you had breakfast yet? We can go to the cafeteria to grab some coffee and talk it over? Peggy?"

Her eyes are brimming with tears. *Crap.* I've overwhelmed her with information. How can I backpedal?

I inhale, an apology perched on my tongue, but clamp my mouth shut when Peggy lifts one finger. I wait as she reads over the proposal once more.

"I think this is a wonderful idea," she finally

says, lifting her gaze from the computer screen.

Hope blossoms in my chest as all my tension dissipates with a big, relieved sigh. "I'm so glad you think so."

I'm so glad, in fact, I could lean over this desk and give her a big, wet kiss on the cheek. Instead, I just give her a wide, goofy smile, practically buzzing with excitement.

Peggy, on the other hand, has wiped away her tears and is all business. "How can I help?" she asks, closing the computer to look at me.

I purse my lips for a moment, thinking. "Well, you have such a wonderful connection with our donors . . . how about this? Today, you can call the donors and tell them about the event and ticket prices. Then you can offer an additional two tickets for only two hundred dollars more. This way, we get more people in the door, more eyes on our auction items, and a little extra money in the bank. How does that sound?"

"I can do that." Peggy nods, already scrolling through the contacts in her phone. She suddenly looks up, concern marking her features again. "Will we have enough time to prepare?"

"We'll do whatever we can with the time we have. After this, I'm going to call a friend about a venue for the evening." Reaching across the desk, I gently squeeze one of Peggy's hands to reassure her. "I promise I'll do everything in my power to save Riverside from collapse."

"If anyone can do it, I think you can, Maren." Her tone is resolute, and I pray she's right about this.

After Peggy marches out the door, a woman on a mission, I pull out my cell phone and call the one person who may be able to take all my big ideas and make something out of them.

"Hey, baby girl, what's up?" Scarlett's voice rings out over the phone. She's chewing on something, most likely the yogurt-and-granola breakfast I know she loves.

"Hey, I was wondering if you could help me with a project," I say, tucking my phone against my shoulder as I turn on my desktop computer.

"Anything you need. I'm your magic lady genie in a bottle."

I chuckle, enjoying that mental image for a moment before diving in. "Okay. What's the likelihood that the Loft will donate space to a well-loved retirement home for a fancy late-summer gala?" Now that I've said it out loud, I can hear how absurd my request is. But Scarlett doesn't skip a beat.

"Depends on the ol' schedge. Give me a sec."

My eyebrows jump in surprise. I was expecting at least a single question or concern. Then I remind myself that as an event coordinator, Scarlett deals with these kinds of inquiries on a daily basis. Lucky for me, and for Riverside, this is her specialty.

"How about early summer instead? We had a wedding cancellation for June twentieth. Sad for them, but fortunate for you."

"June twentieth?" I choke, frantically searching for the date on my calendar. Less than a month away. *Yikes*.

"Yep. Sexy summer solstice. At this point, I doubt we'll find any other renters, and we're definitely keeping their deposit because—I'll say it—screw them and their crappy engagement. So, what do you think?"

I almost want to ask, *Is there* anything *later?* But I bite my tongue. "June twentieth would be perfect. Pencil us in, and let me know what you need from me."

"Sure thing, Mare. I'll send you a contract around lunchtime. I have to rewrite a few things if we aren't going to charge you. Wow, how cool. I'm excited to work with you!" Scarlett giggles between mouthfuls of breakfast, and I happily join in.

"Me too. You're the absolute best."

"Nah, girl. Just make me some cookies, and we'll call it even."

Now it's my turn to cry. "Sure thing."

We say our good-byes, and I spend the next ten minutes browsing through photos of the Loft on their website. It's intimate, it's gorgeous, and it just might do the trick.

I don't want to jinx it . . . but I think this is going to work out, after all. I can't wait to tell Hayes.

Seven

HAYES

"We're looking for something . . . discreet."

"Can't have the kids stumbling across a ten-inch hot pink dildo, now can we?"

Ten inches? Someone's ambitious.

Wolfie and I are at the back of our storefront, balancing spreadsheets. But for the past ten minutes, we've had a front-row seat to Connor attempting to help a middle-aged couple find the perfect toy to spice up their struggling marriage.

He's got his work cut out for him, because judging by the look on the wife's face, visiting us wasn't her idea. Lucky for her, this might be the best thing her husband's ever talked her into. Customer satisfaction is a baseline requirement in this business. And ours is guaranteed.

My friends and I created an ecofriendly line of sex toys. I know you're probably rolling your eyes—five male friends who started a sex-toy company—but we saw a market and wanted to make a difference. It's how Wolfie, Connor, Caleb, Ever, and I found ourselves as the co-owners of Frisky Business. Our toys are couple-focused and female friendly, and our shop has zero creepy vibes.

Connor lets out a good-natured laugh and guides them to our couples corner in the back. We're not like those seedy sex shops you find at the end of a strip mall, full of feathers and mannequins and tacky displays. We're all about the intersection of sophistication and sensuality. Sure, sex sells, but we don't have to be fucking cavemen about it.

"Twenty bucks says he tries to sell them on the Joie de Vivre, and they settle for a basic cock ring," I say under my breath, arching a brow at Wolfie.

He grunts and narrows his eyes at the couple, who are currently doing the *what does this thing do* dance around a particularly well-disguised flesh-light. "No way. She's leaving with an LT."

The Luxe Tube is our bestselling toy. It's small and easy to conceal, but what it lacks in size, it makes up for in strength. With eight powerful vibration settings, it'll leave any woman begging for more. Oh, and the best part? It looks exactly like a luxury tube of lipstick.

"No way the husband goes for that. You're on, man."

Wolfie and I shake on it and discreetly turn our attention back to the couple.

Like I guessed, Connor's pointing them to the Joie de Vivre, a couples toy meant to enhance everyone's experience. It's not quite the dainty, discreet toy the wife claimed to be looking for, but it's not a ten-inch hot-pink dildo either. It also happens to be one of our pricier toys, which is why it's always Connor's go-to recommendation.

Connor has something we all lack. I might wear my heart on my sleeve and get caught up in feelings when I shouldn't, but Connor was born with a big heart. Maybe that's why this is the right job for him—the guy genuinely wants to help people, even if that help is to improve their sex life. He cares. He wants to make the world a better place. And he enjoys talking to people.

Me? I get lost in my head too much, and am too selfish to genuinely care about which toy is right for this couple. Buy both. Or don't. Seriously, I don't care. And I've never been good at small talk.

Although, I guess I'm better at it than Wolfie, who's been known to communicate in grunts and head nods. Connor, on the other hand, puts people at ease. He knows just the right thing to say to break the ice with this couple, probably something witty, because now the three of them are chuckling together.

"Are they . . ." Wolfie trails off, his mouth hanging open.

"Holy shit. They're leaving with the Joie de Vivre."

"What's a Joie de Vivre?" a light, familiar voice asks from behind us, one I wasn't expecting to hear for a while.

Especially not now. Especially not *here*, at work, surrounded by sex toys. With her older brother standing right next to me.

Fuck.

It's Maren, dressed in a pair of yoga pants that hug her curves perfectly and send my mind to all the wrong places. I keep my eyes trained on the couple, who are now at the register with Connor. *Fuck me up the ass.* How the hell am I supposed to get anything done with her here?

"What are you doing here?" Wolfie asks gruffly.

Glad I'm not the only one dying to know the answer to that question.

"Hello to you too, big brother. It's so good to see you. I'm doing just fine, thanks," she says, an irritated smile on her face.

"It's weird that you're here," I blurt.

Wolfie grunts in agreement. "Shouldn't you be at work?"

Realizing that I might know more about Maren's work situation than her brother does at the moment, I search her face for answers but come up blank.

She hardly blinks at Wolfie's question, instead browsing through our displays. Biting her lip, she wanders a few steps down an aisle filled with anal plugs in varying sizes and colors.

My cock twitches at the sight of her fingers on one of the toys. *This is going to be worse than I thought.*

"I worked from home today," she says and looks directly at me. "And I'm actually here on business."

Wolfie looks between us, confused, and my stomach drops. The last thing I need is for him to be suspicious of something between me and Maren.

"You're looking to enter the toy industry?" he asks.

Maren rolls her eyes. "Hayes is helping me with a fundraiser for Riverside."

Wolfie's eyebrows shoot up, and I don't even want to think about where his mind might be going. He looks at me and crosses his arms.

Doing my best to play it off casually, I shrug. "You told me to check on your sister, and it snowballed from there."

He returns my shrug and tucks a pen behind his ear. "Always the knight in shining armor."

I don't miss the tinge of sarcasm in his tone. He knows something's up, but he's letting it go. And right now, that's my only saving grace.

"Holy shit. Maren Cox? Are you finally ready to let me sell you the vibrator that will change your life?" Connor appears next to Maren and loops his arm around her waist.

The dude's pissed me off before, but never like this. The sight of Connor's bulky forearm around her narrow waist gives me heart palpitations. *Not cool.* I'm about ready to rip his face off if he doesn't take his hands off her in the next five seconds.

From the looks of it, I'm not the only one. Wolfie's nostrils flare, and he looks about ready to sock Connor into next weekend.

Maren giggles nervously. "I was actually wondering if you could tell me what the Joie de Vivre is? These two apparently went deaf when I asked about it."

Connor gives her a smile that makes me want to rip his balls off and shove them down his throat. "Wait right here."

Within moments, he returns with an armful of toys and lays them out on the table in front of her. Her eyes grow wide, and when she starts rifling through them, flicking some on and gasping when they light up or vibrate, my jaw about falls straight to the floor. This is downright unfair.

Connor places the sleek U-shaped toy in her hands, his smile widening. "The Joie de Vivre can be used in any position, though I recommend couples try missionary to start. It's also very effective solo," he adds with a wink.

Wolfie lets out a long, irritated breath from beside me.

Welcome to the fucking club, dude.

I can't tell which is worse—watching Connor flirt with Maren, or watching Maren fondle a sex toy. My mind keeps flashing with wild fantasies, and my heart is pounding in my throat.

Her hands move to our collection of vibrators in various shapes—hearts, cylinders, shells. One even looks like a gummy bear. When she finds the Luxe Tube in the pile, she twists it open, a small smile forming on her lips.

"Now this one I'm familiar with," she says, giving me a look dripping with sin.

Not. Fucking. Fair.

I clench my jaw and take a deep breath. She's playing with me. That much is clear. What a sexy little sadist.

Without breaking eye contact, she presses the **ON** button and the motor starts to hum. "Mmm. Very familiar," she purrs.

Wolfie snatches the tube out of her hands and turns it off. "It's not a fucking toy."

A laugh falls from her perfect lips. "That's literally what it is."

"You know what I mean. Just. Stop. It," he says, playing every bit the stern older brother he is.

"I'm just curious," she says innocently.

Wolfie narrows his eyes and goes back to his computer, grumbling under his breath.

"What about this one?" she asks, holding up a

thick black cylinder with a pink latex lining. She runs her fingertip along the edge, and I feel a strain behind my zipper.

"That one's for our male customers," Connor says with a sly grin, raking his fingers through his dark blond hair. "You could make a guy really happy by pulling that out in the bedroom."

Her gaze flits to mine, and my pants tighten even more.

My mind goes completely blank, except for every single thought that I'm not supposed to think. Kissing down her stomach to her bare, shaven pussy. Pushing my length into her. Watching her suck my—

"Are you having a fucking stroke?" Wolfie asks, his voice snapping me out of my trance.

I swear I catch Maren smile, her lips twitching at my obvious discomfort, before I turn to Wolfie and try to act like I wasn't just fucking his kid sister in my mind.

"Sorry, I spaced out."

"Caleb's on the phone. He wants to make sure we're still on for the lake house this weekend." Wolfie's flustered. His jaw ticks as he waits for my response.

"Yep. Leaving bright and early Saturday morning." Thankfully, my voice comes out even.

"The lake's going to be fucking sick, man. I can't wait," Connor says, placing another toy in Maren's hands.

I nod. It's tradition for all of us to head to my family's lake house every year, and this one's no different. We've got a whole weekend of drinking, swimming, and bonfires ahead of us.

"Tell your grandma thanks again for letting us stay at her place. I'm dying for some time away," Maren says, giving me an appreciative look.

I nod and look away. If the other toys were too much to handle, watching her hold an anatomically correct, flesh-colored dildo in her hands is where I draw the line. It's impossible to stop myself from imagining pumping the toy into her, watching her squirm as—

"Hayes, do you have the numbers from last quarter? Some of this shit just won't reconcile," Wolfie grumbles, furrowing his brow at the computer.

Numbers. Spreadsheets. These are what I should be focusing on.

I clear my throat, thinking that maybe putting

some distance between Maren and me will help. "Yeah, let me run to the back and grab my laptop."

I walk quickly to the back of the storefront where we have a small supply closet, a few rows of back stock, and another few hundred square feet of office space. When I reach my desk, the door to the back swings open again, and footsteps approach.

"Look, Wolfie, I know I've got the numbers here somewhere, all right? Just give me a minute."

But the voice that answers isn't Wolfie's. It's Maren's.

"I was, uh, hoping we could talk about the auction?" She stands awkwardly on the other side of my desk, the dildo still in her hand. When she catches me staring at it, she holds it up with a small, mischievous smile. "I'm not trying to steal it or anything. I just wanted to catch a moment alone with you."

Why do our conversations always start out like the beginning of a porno?

I take a seat and gesture for her to sit down. Instead of sitting in one of the chairs next to my desk, though, she rests her ass on the edge of it, much closer than I was expecting.

She sets the dildo down in front of me. "I was

wondering if maybe you could put together a basket for the auction," she says, her eyes lowered to her hands.

"Sure, I can find a suitable vendor and work out a contract. It'll be easy."

"No, I meant *you*. As in the company. I'd ask Wolfie, but even the thought is too mortifying."

"You want to sell a basket of adult toys . . . to old people?" I try to keep my tone as measured as possible. I want to help her—more than I probably should—but this is one thing I'm not so sure about.

"I know it sounds crazy, but we'll be inviting people from all over, from all walks of life. Plus, *old people* are more sexually active than you'd think."

"Okay, not a mental image I ever wanted in my head."

We laugh, and she places her hand over mine.

"Everyone likes orgasms," she says softly, making my heart rate rachet even higher.

My mouth has gone dry, and I've forgotten how to form a response that isn't just a helpless noise of agreement. *Good times*.

But Maren is as polished as ever. Crossing one

ankle over the other and tipping her chin, she says, "Just think about it, okay? I don't need an answer right now."

I nod, trying to ignore the extra blood flow to my crotch.

"Oh, and Hayes?"

"Yeah?"

"Thank you again. For everything. I really don't know how I'm going to make it all up to you." She glances from the dildo to my lap, then up to my face. "But I'm excited for the lake house this weekend."

She turns and walks away. With no one else around to see me, I watch her ass as she leaves, and I swear she knows it.

Honestly, I don't really know what just happened. But I do know I want to find out.

Eight

MAREN

The morning sun shines through the windshield of Wolfie's car, casting warmth across my freckled shoulders. Wind whips through the open windows as my brother speeds down the highway, the radio forecast promising beautiful weather for the weekend ahead.

Trailing behind us is Caleb in his Jeep, with Scarlett in the front seat, and Connor and his little sister Penelope squashed together in the back. If I sit up straight, I can see Scarlett in the rearview mirror, jamming to whatever playlist she's forcing the rest of the car to endure.

For a moment, I regret opting to ride with my brother. I love him, but Wolfie isn't the easiest guy to talk to, especially if you're sitting in a car with him for almost three hours. Lucky for me, I wasn't the only one who opted for a quieter road trip.

Am I lucky, though? Truthfully, I can't decide how I feel about being crammed in this small space with Hayes riding shotgun.

I was reluctant to leave Chicago in the first place, what with all my obligations surrounding the fundraiser. But now, with the promise of actual downtime and sunbathing, I'm grateful that Wolfie and Scarlett insisted I come along.

Trying to chase away any fleeting worries, I close my eyes. Maybe I can sleep for the rest of the car ride, and then when I wake up, I'll already be in Saugatuck. There's no such thing as work in Saugatuck—not with the beach calling my name.

With my eyes closed, my sense of smell is heightened. It's not just the sweet aroma of fresh air that's stirring excitement in me. It's Hayes and his clean, masculine scent that always makes me dizzy with desire.

Giving in to my curiosity, I open my eyes and sneak a glance at him.

Hayes stares out the windshield, his sharp eyes focused on the road ahead of us. In the sunlight, they look like liquid gold. Somehow he's already perfected his summer tan, evident by his sculpted forearm resting against the armrest. I find myself staring at his long fingers, tapping to the beat of the song on the radio against the leather of the car seat.

When he glances in the rearview mirror and catches me staring, I struggle to spit out an excuse.

"Do . . . do you like this song?"

I pinch my leg, hard. Where's the button that will eject my seat straight into the stratosphere?

"Never heard it before," Hayes mutters with an apathetic shrug, grumpier than one ought to be on his way to his family's lake house. Crappy mood or not, he's still gorgeous.

I hum along to the music, grateful this conversation ended before I could embarrass myself any further. I catch Wolfie's eyes, watching me from the rearview mirror. I offer him a nonchalant smile and immediately avert my gaze.

Yes, this blurry scenery whizzing past is very, very interesting.

No, I'm not concerned that my big brother is on to me, suspecting the crush I have on his best friend and business partner.

Hayes seems to be completely oblivious to my interest in him, thank God. And I seriously doubt Wolfie has any suspicions. As sharp as his insight may be into all things business-related, he's pretty blind to anything involving emotions. Unlike me, who's constantly consumed with them.

I'm so lost in thought that I don't realize we've arrived at our destination until the car comes to a stop. I sit up straight, eager to get out of the car and stretch my legs.

I've been to Hayes's family lake house before, but it's even more beautiful than I remember. The dark, rustic exterior is surrounded on three sides by strikingly tall shade trees. The porch wraps around the house, providing plenty of space for the whole group to hang out and enjoy a cocktail, or for some introverted quality time alone on the porch swing.

My favorite part is the glimmering view of Lake Michigan, only thirty or so yards from the house. If you step off the porch and onto the deck, you have an unobstructed view of the path that winds down to the beach and its miraculously blue water.

"Coming through." Hayes breezes by me, the straps of both of our duffels in one hand and a twelve-pack of beer in the other.

"You don't have to carry mine," I call out, jogging to keep up with him. There must have been rain last night, because my shoes sink in the muddied gravel of the driveway with every step.

"Don't tell me you forgot the keys," Wolfie

says, his voice classically stern. He's already at the door, sitting on top of a cooler and looking all kinds of impatient.

I'm sure no one will forget the year Hayes forgot the keys anytime soon. A neighbor saw us breaking in through a window and called the police. It took Hayes almost twenty minutes to convince them that it's actually his grandma's house.

"Shit," Hayes mutters, then turns to me. "Keys are in my pocket. Wanna help a guy out? Unless you don't mind mud on your bag."

"Oh, um, I'll get them. Which pocket?"

"Left front."

Do not think about his penis, don't think about it, don't think about it, don't think about it.

Slipping my hand into his pocket, I do my best to ignore the hard angle of his hip bone, the firm muscle of his thigh, the heady scent of his skin so close to mine. I fish the keys out, a single ring holding two simple keys—front door and back door, I assume.

When I meet Hayes's eyes again, he's completely unfazed, no hint of emotion in their honey depths. Based on the burning of my cheeks, I must look like a tomato. I turn away quickly, tossing the keys to Wolfie and jogging back to the car to find any remaining groceries to bring inside.

Caleb's Jeep rolls across the gravel driveway to join us. Out hops Scarlett, her arms outstretched for a hug. I could use a little Scarlett energy this weekend.

"Hi, baby." She sighs happily into my ear, rocking us side to side.

"Hi." I chuckle, squeezing her tight. "This is going to be a fun weekend."

"Hell yeah, it is!"

Moments later, Penelope and I are tag-teaming a cooler up the steps of the porch. With a final huff, we drop the cooler in front of the door, exchanging triumphant smiles. That's when I hear the crunch of tires on the gravel again.

Who else is coming?

Out of a midsize blue sedan slides a pair of long, tanned legs. Wearing a long summer maxi dress and with raven-black hair cascading over her shoulders, a woman looks up, meeting my eyes with a smile and a wave. It takes me a moment to place her, and I'm caught staring.

"Hi, Maren. Do you remember me?" Slinging her bag over her shoulder and hiking up her skirt, she walks toward us.

Oh, I remember her. Too vividly, perhaps.

Behind me, I hear the swing of the front door as Hayes steps out of the house, muttering under his breath, "What the fuck . . ."

"Who is that?" Penelope asks, her big, innocent eyes filled with questions.

In record time, I'm able to swallow the lump in my throat and smile back. "Holly, right? It's been a long time. How are you?" I ask, but what I'm thinking is, *What are you doing here?*

Hayes, tactless as ever, asks the unspoken question. "What are you doing here, Holly?"

Her matte-red lips twist into a pout. "Don't be mean, Hayes. I know you missed me. Oh, hey, Wolfie. How are you, handsome?"

Before I can register Wolfie's presence, Holly is bounding up the steps to wrap him in a gigantic bear hug. Since when is Wolfie friends with Hayes's ex? Ex is a stretch . . . They were friends with benefits for years.

Out of all the women that passed through the revolving door of his bedroom, Holly was the only regular. She was the only girl Hayes ever had a consistent fling with, something that lasted years, not weeks or months like all the others.

Is it too late to go back to the city?

"Hey, Holly," Wolfie grumbles in his typical way, patting her on the back. That's his cue to say, *I'm done with this hug, thank you.*

I almost want to laugh, but I have too many questions. Did Hayes invite her? Is she staying for the whole weekend? Where is she going to sleep?

"Wolfie and I were just about to clean the grill. If you'll excuse us," Hayes says tersely, looking annoyed.

If he didn't know Holly was coming . . . then who invited her?

Hayes plants a hand on the back of Wolfie's neck, steering him around the side of the house and out of sight. Penelope's brows furrow with confusion, but Holly's smile hasn't budged. It's more of a smirk, really. She clearly thinks she's won something, or she will win something—or *someone*—by being here.

My stomach twists into a painful knot. It's already hard enough being around Hayes, but to have to watch his fuck-buddy stake her claim and paw all over him this weekend will be freaking torture.

"Would you like to come inside?" I hear myself

asking, one hand outstretched in an offer to take her bag. *What am I, a butler?* "I can give you a quick tour."

"Thanks, but I've been here plenty of times before," she says with a wink before slipping between Penelope and me and disappearing into the house.

My heart hammers in my ears as mild frustration threatens to transform into a full-on rage. Penelope must sense my discomfort because she reaches out and gives my hand a comforting squeeze before she follows Holly inside.

I'm not ready to go in, not with Holly there. Instead, I tiptoe around the side of the house until I can hear the deep voices of Hayes and Wolfie.

"Are you fucking kidding me, man? How could you invite her?"

A surge of relief passes through me. Hayes isn't happy that Holly is here. He's *pissed.*

"Look, she reached out to me. She made it sound like you two were seeing each other again."

"What the hell? We're not." Hayes's tone is biting, while my brother sounds more apologetic.

"Fuck, man. I'm sorry. I would have asked you, but you'd sworn off women, and I didn't want to start a whole damn intervention."

Wolfie really does sound sorry. He knows he messed up.

"Fuck, it's okay, man. We'll figure it out." Hayes heaves out a sigh, the anger in his voice deflating into tired resignation.

Maybe it's the problem-solver in me, but I want to help. I knock softly on the side of the house as I step into view, trying not to startle anyone.

Hayes's eyes snap to mine, a flurry of fiery emotion suddenly turning to ice. "What's up, Mare?"

"Is there anything I can do? I overheard that Holly . . . was a surprise."

Hayes laughs without humor, rubbing his forehead. "Yeah, no shit," he mumbles, turning his back to me.

Why won't he look at me?

"Would you mind rooming with her? That would help a lot," my brother asks, placing a hand on my shoulder and giving it a squeeze.

My throat tightens. I wasn't expecting that. Rooming with Holly will be . . . a challenge. But if I can make this awkward tension any easier on Hayes, I will. Also, if I can keep her out of Hayes's bedroom—all the better, right?

"Sure thing." I smile, but it probably doesn't reach my eyes.

Hayes mutters something under his breath and stalks off.

A few minutes later, we have the rooming situation finalized.

Penelope and Scarlett will take the queen bed in the downstairs bedroom, and I'll take the bunk-bed situation with Holly. Wolfie will room with Connor in the double-twin room, since they already have that roommate dynamic. Caleb will take the couch, and Hayes will sleep in his own room.

Which just so happens to share a hallway with my sleeping arrangement.

I make the decision to avoid fantasizing about any late-night visits from a man who clearly will never see me as more than his best friend's little sister. If anything's going to happen tonight, it'll be between Holly and Hayes, a thought that stings like burning-hot metal slicing into my skin.

Inside, Wolfie and Hayes call a brief assembly of all the lake-house guests to lay down the arrangements and some ground rules—no smoking in the house, shoes off the carpet, et cetera.

"Any questions?" Hayes asks, scanning the

room.

"Yes!" Holly chirps, raising her hand. "Who wants to go to the beach with me?"

Caleb, Connor, Penelope, and Scarlett raise their hands in response, a murmur of approval floating throughout the room. I begrudgingly raise my own hand. The smirk plastered on my face is as believable as it's gonna get.

Twenty minutes later, we're all suited up and walking down the path toward the water. Hayes took off first with Holly close on his tail, so I hang back with Wolfie.

"Are you okay?" I ask him, worried that this trip is already ruined for him because of the snafu with Holly.

"Yeah, I'm good," he says. "Sometimes I wish Hayes would just commit to one person. Then shit like this wouldn't happen."

I avert my gaze, glancing down at the sand peeking through the gravel. "Me too."

A bit of a distance ahead of us, Penelope's laughter carries on the breeze while Scarlett gesticulates wildly, probably telling another dating-app story. Most of us are wearing some sort of wrap or cover-up, but Penelope walks confidently in her cute blue bikini. She looks absolutely adorable, her high ponytail bouncing with each step.

"I'm so glad Penelope is finally twenty-one, you know? I feel like we can really let loose together and—"

I lose track of what I'm saying, my train of thought completely cut off by the bewildering expression on my brother's face. He's flushed, and his eyes are glued to . . . oh my God, is he staring at Penelope's *ass*?

I elbow him hard in the side.

"What?" he grumbles, rubbing his ribs.

"Subtlety, man. You need some."

Just as Wolfie is about to argue his defense, Caleb barrels past us in a sprint, carrying two flip-flops that most definitely do not belong to him. Calling over his shoulder, he yells, "Last one to the beach loses his flippy-floppers!"

Seconds later, Connor bolts by us, barefoot, chasing after Caleb like his life depends on it. "I only brought one pair! Fuck you, man! Fuck you!"

I chuckle, watching their bromance unfold.

By the time Wolfie and I have caught up, Connor is tackling Caleb in the water, a battle that I can only assume will end with someone—at worst—getting a black eye, or—at best—getting water up his nose.

Scarlett and Penelope lay out their towels, completely ignoring the splash fest ahead of them. Holly, on the other hand, is putting on a whole show of removing her wrap, tie by tie, revealing a white-bikini-clad body that belongs on a magazine and *not* at this lake house. She's making eyes in Hayes's general direction, but as I follow her gaze, I'm pleased to see that he's otherwise occupied.

A few trees stand nearby, one carrying more memories than the others. A thick rope swing hangs far across the water, where the sand drops off and the water gets deep and dark. As a kid, I was barely brave enough to swing over the water, refusing to jump off despite Wolfie and Hayes's jeering. Now, the guys are taking turns, flying over the water, hitting the surface with a splash, and finally coming up for air.

The sight of them reminds me of when we were all teenagers. Only now, Hayes is taller, more muscular, and even more beautiful than I ever could have imagined he'd become. Despite my best efforts, he's the man I always compared my past relationships to. And somehow they never measured up. Hayes always made me feel safe. And when I lost my parents . . . he was there for me. I've always depended on him. Always wanted more of him.

A low twinge hits my belly and a shiver runs up my spine. How long have I felt this way about him? How long have I wanted to lick water droplets off his skin?

Watching him walk ashore again, it's impossible to tear my gaze away. That wide, sculpted chest. Those bulky forearms that I long to feel around me. The tight ass that presses enticingly against his swim trunks with each deliberate stride. Arousal—hot and insistent—courses through my veins.

"Hey, girl, why are you just standing there?"

Scarlett's voice snaps me back to reality, and I turn to see her looking at me, sunglasses pushed low on her nose.

"Want to hang with us?" she asks, waving me over.

My cheeks are still burning, and the throbbing in my core hasn't subsided one bit. I need to cool off first.

"After a swim. I'll be right back."

I whip off the oversized T-shirt I've used for years as a cover-up, finally allowing the sun to kiss my exposed shoulders and belly. My bathing suit was a clearance find at the local department store. The halter top is black with crocheted teal overlay, complementing my naturally pale skin and cradling my breasts comfortably. The high-waisted bottoms I wear are black, with a teal braided belt around my hips.

I don't stop to check if Hayes notices my new suit. Instead, I take off toward the dock and dive in. The water is absolutely freezing, but I don't care. It's exactly what I need to cool down.

Once I'm submerged, my thoughts finally quiet. With each stroke, I distance myself from my worries and insecurities. I'd forgotten how much I love swimming. I wonder if there's a gym near my apartment that I could—

Something grasps my foot, startling me, and I pull myself above water, kicking wildly. "Whoa, whoa, whoa!"

To my complete shock, it's Hayes, treading water near me. His hair is soaked, tiny droplets falling onto his cheekbones. My heart hammers, and I wish I could say it was just from the shock.

"What are you doing?" I demand, splashing him.

"I just wanted to catch up to you before you got too far." He laughs, splashing me back. "Don't be mad, dove."

One side of his mouth lifts in a crooked smile, and the anger in me melts into something gooey and warm.

"Aww, were you worried about me, Hayes?" I splash him again, this time more teasingly.

"Maybe I was." He eyes me with a hypnotic grin. "Splash me one more time. I dare you."

I bite my lip, mock-deliberating my options. With a laugh, I lean back into the water, splashing him repeatedly with the kicking of my feet.

"Oh, that's it," he says, his voice low but playful.

With that, Hayes tackles me, pulling me down beneath the surface with him. As one of his hands wraps tightly around my ankle, and the other snakes behind my back, I'm suddenly pressed up against him in all sorts of intimate ways. My body reacts before I can think straight, my arms wrapping around those broad shoulders with an urgency I've never been able to act on before.

Maren, don't give anything away.

But then, the strangest of things happens. I feel something long and thick hardening against my thigh.

When we resurface, my arms are still locked

around his shoulders, my breasts pressed against his slick, bare chest. Our eyes meet, his whiskey-colored gaze sending a hot rush through me. His fingers squeeze my waist as I'm pressed firmly against his rather impressive erection.

"Hayes . . ."

Abruptly, he removes my arms from his neck. Without his support, I tread water again easily, but Hayes doesn't stick around.

I rock with the waves of his departure, watching his muscular arms slice through the water as he swims back to the others. He pulls himself up and onto the dock, not pausing even for Holly, who attempts to intercept him on his way back to the house.

What just happened?

Nine

HAYES

What. The. Actual. Fuck. Bro.

If I were an emoji, I'd be the screaming face with steam coming out of his ears.

There was no denying Maren felt my body's response to hers. And I could tell the second she did. One minute we were splashing around in the water, and the next, her soft curves were pressed up close as her wet skin made contact with mine. Then it was game over. I needed to put as much distance as possible between us, so I fled without another word or a backward glance.

I stalk up the stairs and slam the door once I'm inside my room.

My dick still so rock hard, I desperately need to jerk off. I tug open the front of my swim shorts and give myself a warning squeeze. I'm gonna blow way too soon at this rate.

But an errant thought stops me dead in my tracks.

What if Wolfie saw me flirting with his sister, and he's on his way up here right now to confront me? I certainly don't want him to walk in and see me with my dick in my hand. Talk about being caught red-handed.

With my knuckles turning white as I grip the edge of the dresser, I hang my head and try to breathe. Abandoning my earlier plan, I lace up my swim shorts and blow out another sigh.

Wolfie is a cock block, and he doesn't even fucking know it. Plus, he invited Holly. It's a testament to how clueless he is about how I feel about his sister that he thought I'd want Holly here.

Deciding I can't jack off, I take a deep, calming breath and attempt to give myself a pep talk.

Just get through tonight. That's all you have to do.

This is fucking torture, and I'm not just talking about my body's physical response to Maren's. This entire game is torture. The desire to touch her and tease her until she's smiling . . . I want it all.

But I have no other choice than to pretend there's nothing happening between us.

Deciding to carry on as though everything is normal, I change into a dry pair of shorts and a T-shirt, then go downstairs and begin preparing food for dinner. When everyone comes back from the water in an hour or two, hungry and slightly tipsy, I'll have everything ready. Hopefully, the need for food will distract them from asking why I ditched the water.

I marinate steaks and form ground beef into a dozen burgers. But keeping my hands busy does little to calm my mind. I can't stop thinking about what Wolfie would say if he knew how I felt. Most likely, he'd scowl at me and cite my awful track record with women as the reason why he'd never support the idea of me and Maren.

When I've sliced limes and added margarita mix to the blender, the screen door opens and the first few of the crew filter inside. Caleb and Connor are bickering about something, while Scarlett and Penelope are talking about which one is going to shower first.

Holly makes a pleased sound when she sees me working in the kitchen. She was always that way, exuberant about the smallest things. After she steals a handful of potato chips, she thankfully disappears upstairs.

I keep my eyes downcast on my task so I don't have to look at Maren right now. I have maybe an hour, tops, until everyone remerges freshly showered and no longer sandy, and then I'll have no choice but to face her. And I have no idea how to apologize for what happened in the water.

"You okay?" a husky voice asks from behind me.

I turn and see Wolfie, his expression impassive. While that's not abnormal for him, part of me wishes he were smiling, that he'd give me some signal to let me know we're okay and that he's not secretly planning my demise. But that's not Wolfie, and I can't expect him to change his stripes just to appease my fragile ego.

"Yeah," I lie. "Fine. Just thought I'd make myself useful."

I'm stiff and can't meet his eyes, but Wolfie doesn't call me on my bullshit. Instead, he just nods.

It's tradition for me to grill our first night here, so this isn't out of the ordinary. Me spending all of fifteen minutes at the beach, however, *is* unheard of.

But Wolfie doesn't call me on it, and for that I'm grateful. I'm not sure how much longer I can keep lying to him, but I have to. I have to act normal and try to carry on, have to laugh with my friends. And most importantly, I have to keep my eyes off Maren's tits in her bikini top.

To be honest, I'm not sure how it's possible that Wolfie doesn't know. I feel like every emotion and bolt of lust I have about Maren must be written all over my face.

It turns out, grilling for everyone is the perfect thing to do with my hands since they can't be used for the thing I most desire—groping Maren's curves. When the food is done, everyone grabs a plate and lines up at the grill on the back deck. Donning a spatula and a smile, I serve up the food. All I'm missing is a chef's hat and apron.

Maren is one of the last through the line, and when I place the portabella mushroom burger I made just for her onto her plate, she smiles, and I notice how soft her eyes are as she looks at me.

"Thanks, Hayes."

"Of course." I nod once.

She doesn't budge. "Are you okay?"

"I'm fine."

She shifts, looking uncertain. "If I did something wrong back at the beach . . ."

"You didn't," I say quickly. "I'm sorry I ran off like that." I look down, flipping a burger that doesn't need turning, just so I have something to do with my hands.

"So, you're not mad at me?" she asks, her voice low.

A pang of guilt zings through me. "No, of course not."

The last thing I wanted to do was make her feel bad. None of this is her fault.

Before I can figure out how to articulate any of that, Holly appears out of nowhere.

"Can I talk to you?" She meets my eyes with a serious expression.

I open my mouth to reply, but Maren is ducking away with her food, heading off to join her brother and Penelope at the picnic table situated on the lawn under a cluster of birch trees.

"Sure," I say, grabbing a plate for myself.

"Somewhere private," Holly adds.

With renewed patience, I turn off the gas to the grill and carry my plate, following Holly around the side of the house. She stops to lean on the porch railing, setting her plate aside.

"If my being here is a distraction, I'm sorry. I didn't mean to cause any problems."

"It's fine, Holly. I just . . ." I release a slow breath. "A heads-up would have been nice."

I haven't seen or spoken to Holly in more than six months. Once upon a time, we filled a void in each other's lives. But that was a long time ago. Our chemistry was good . . . until it wasn't.

Holly made it clear she wasn't interested in settling down and popping out a few kids. Which was fine, at first. But when I realized our goals were never going to align, I lost interest. She was fun and easy to be with, but I knew I wanted more than just a good time.

Eventually, I wanted a real commitment. A family. And that just wasn't Holly. But I couldn't blame her for that. She knew what she wanted and was honest about it.

But coming here today at Wolfie's merest suggestion? It's typical Holly, always down for a good time. Maybe she thought I'd be single and horny, and we could just pick up right where we left off.

Hell, maybe that's why Wolfie invited her,

thinking I needed to take the edge off with some casual sex. Too bad that's the last thing I need right now. I need to focus, and *not* be thinking with my dick. Especially since it seems intent in getting me in trouble.

Holly nods. "Are you seeing anyone?"

I set my plate down beside hers and pinch the bridge of my nose. "Can we just not do this?"

With a manicured hand on her hip, she gives me a pointed look. "Calm down, Hayes. I'm not trying to start something that you're not into."

I inhale and nod. "Good."

She laughs and shakes her head at me. "Way to dodge the question."

"I'm single right now, and that's the way I want it to stay."

"Understood." She smiles at me. "If you change your mind, you know where to find me."

My expression stays blank while Holly continues grinning.

Fucking Holly. I don't want her getting any ideas about us. This is the last goddamn thing I need right now.

Ignoring the *I'm down to fuck if you are* gleam

in her eyes, I grab my plate. With one last nod in her direction, I stalk away to find someplace quiet to eat.

Miraculously, I manage to successfully avoid Maren for the next few hours.

When she's inside with Scarlett and Penelope tackling the dishes, I'm outside starting the bonfire. When she's lying in the hammock on the porch with a book, I'm upstairs taking a shower.

Now I'm sitting outside in a lawn chair near the fire with a cold beer.

"Nice job on the fire," Scarlett says, rubbing her hands together as she leans closer to the warm glow. Chairs are scattered in a circle, around the fire and everyone is here except for Maren. I have no idea where she is or why she hasn't joined us.

Holly is sitting directly across from me, her eyes daring me to come over there and ravage her. *Not fucking likely.*

Connor and Wolfie are bickering about whose cannonball into the lake was more epic, and I've just started to feel settled when Maren joins the bonfire.

She glances around, quickly noticing that all the chairs are occupied. Then she looks my way and moves closer. "Is this seat taken?"

I'm about to get up and offer her my chair when Maren casually plops down in my lap like it's the most natural thing in the world. Although for Maren, maybe it is normal, because she's always been a touchy-feeling type of person. For me, the feeling is . . . unsettling, because I can never seem to wrangle my body under control with her this close.

I mutter something inarticulate as she proceeds to use me as a chair. Wolfie grumbles something under his breath, and I stare into the fire, trying to focus on anything but the way she feels in my lap.

For a moment, I think that I can do this, but the soft weight of her ass pressing into my groin quickly becomes too much. The scent of her shampoo makes my heart rate accelerate, and my body starts to respond. My cock swells, and I'm sure Maren's about to notice.

When I shift her weight, she meets my eyes, and I can't help but notice the challenge in her expression. It's the same feeling that I got when she came to visit the store. We share a silent moment, neither of us looking away. She knows exactly what she's doing to me, so why isn't she moving away?

I'm so distracted and on edge that I can barely focus on the conversations happening around us.

After a little while, a couple of people wander off, ready for bed, and pretty soon, only a few of us are left.

"I think I'm going to turn in," I say.

Maren rises from my lap and gives Wolfie a hug good night. "Me too," she says, giving me a heated look.

I grab the empty beer bottle from beside my chair and give Wolfie and Connor a fist bump. "You guys will make sure the fire's out?"

Connor nods. "We got you."

I wish I could douse my raging attraction to Maren the same way they'll douse the fire.

"Thanks for grilling," Wolfie says.

"My pleasure. Night, guys."

Maren is already heading up the steps and into the house. I follow her, but linger in the kitchen while she climbs the stairs to the bedrooms. The last thing I need right now after that sexually charged bonfire encounter is an awkward hallway run-in with her.

After several minutes, I finally make my way

upstairs and pause at the top. The door to Holly and Maren's shared bedroom is closed, but so is the bathroom door, light escaping from under it. I hear the water running and guess it's Maren brushing her teeth.

Inside my bedroom, I strip out of the clothes that now smell like a campfire and quickly rinse off in the shower. After putting on a clean pair of boxer shorts, I pull back the blankets and climb into bed.

When it's finally quiet and I'm sinking deep into the mattress, I realize something is very, very wrong. The sound of feminine moaning is coming from the bedroom next door, and it's loud. Really loud.

What the fuck?

I know that voice. It's Holly, and she sounds like she's really enjoying herself, maybe even a little too much. But with who?

I climb out of bed and venture out into the hallway to investigate. But when I open the door, I stop short because Maren is standing there, looking as confused as I feel, dressed only in a T-shirt that barely covers her panties.

The moans turn to pants, then screams.

My wide eyes meet Maren's. "Is that . . ."

"Holly," she says.

"But with who?"

"I was in the bathroom when it started. I figured you went in there." Her voice is soft, almost tentative, and she drops her gaze to the floor.

"God, no. I have no interest in her."

Maren's posture changes, her back straightening. It draws up the T-shirt an inch higher, so I can see the front of her panties now. They're soft white cotton. I want to peel them off her with my teeth.

"Well, if you're not in there, who is?"

I shrug. "I think it's just her."

At this, Maren's eyes widen. "Is she trying to make you jealous?"

I shake my head. "No, I think she's trying to make *you* jealous."

Maren's brows draw together. "I don't understand."

I lick my lips, trying to shake off the strange vibe that's filling the hallway. The moaning hasn't stopped. Not even close. "Holly always thought I had a thing for you. Maybe she wants you to think that she and I are in that room."

Maren laughs nervously at the suggestion that I had a thing for her. "Well, that's obviously not true."

My throat dries out, and I don't say anything else. Maren shifts nervously, tugging her T-shirt lower.

After a beat of awkward silence, I say, "Come on, you can bunk with me." What choice do I have? She can't exactly stand in the hallway all night.

Maren follows me inside the bedroom, dark but for the moonlight. We lie down cautiously, each taking a side of the bed, and I give her as much space as I can, careful not to make inadvertent contact.

I have no idea how I'm going to keep my hands to myself. I really should have rubbed one out earlier when I had the chance.

There's one small blessing, though. It seems that Holly has ended her performance. I can't believe her, and I really don't know what I ever saw in her.

Now that it's quiet again, my heart is pounding so hard, I have no idea how Maren doesn't hear it.

Just then, she turns toward me. "I can't sleep," she whispers. "Can you?"

"No."

With the softest featherlight touch, Maren reaches out, placing her fingertips against my jaw. Slowly, she turns my face toward hers. Our eyes meet in the darkness, and I'm still trying to make sense of the heat I see reflected back at me when she leans in and kisses me.

It's the smallest movement—at first. Just the soft brush of her full mouth against mine.

But then I shift, pushing up on my elbow to lean over her, and Maren responds with a small, pleased sound. Her mouth is hungry and hot and moving against mine, making endorphins flood my system.

When I part my lips and her tongue slides easily inside, my entire body jolts at how good it feels. Her warm mouth is incredible.

My brain is a scrambled mess of lust and want. Heat and emotion.

I should leave. But as my control quickly crumbles, I give in and touch her cheek, angling her chin so I can taste more of her. I'm shocked at my actions, but her mouth feels too good to stop, and soon I'm drowning in her.

Taking a deep breath, I fight to get myself under control, but it's useless. She's ruined me.

Heat pulses between us. I tilt her chin, and with my other hand, give my balls a warning squeeze beneath the blankets. It does fuck all to cool me off.

Wolfie wouldn't care that Maren was the one who came on to me. He'd only know that I betrayed him. And that's what this would be. Despite how right it feels—and believe me, right now it feels really fucking right—it would be a complete and utter betrayal of twenty years of friendship.

Desire rips the air from my lungs. I'm not easily shaken, but this . . .

I struggle to stay in control, knowing I should leave. Flee the bed, the room, the lake house, and put as much distance as possible between Maren and me.

Instead, I completely give in. Nothing matters now except for getting inside her. Her breath catches, and she makes another desire-filled sound.

Indecision paralyzes me, a sharp ache inside my chest.

Leave. Stop this now, my brain begs.

The thought of having to look Wolfie in the eye and tell him I defiled his sister is the only thing that can curb the desire ripping me apart like a bomb. I can't. Won't.

She straddles me, and the contact of her warmth pressed over my hard cock is heaven.

Oh fuck. Maybe just for a few minutes more.

What the actual hell, Hayes?

"Dove," I rasp out, breathless and rock hard. "Hold up."

She pulls back to meet my eyes in the glow of pale moonlight filling the room.

"We can't."

With a nod and her chin tucked to her chest, Maren makes a noise of agreement. "I know. I'm sorry." She moves from my lap.

"It's just . . ."

"I understand." Her expression incredibly sad, she slips from the bed and disappears out of my room and into the hall.

She might say she understands, but her expression says otherwise. She's hurt, and I'm the one who caused it.

I can't erase from my brain the look in her eyes when I told her we couldn't.

Shit.

Maren didn't understand anything. She thought I was rejecting her, but the opposite is true. I was protecting her.

And now I have no choice but to go after her.

Ten

MAREN

It takes every ounce of resolve left in me not to cry.

I steady myself against the door, staring at the wall between Hayes's room and mine—well, Holly's. Her little performance—the thumping and moaning—has stopped, but she's claimed her territory.

Besides, I don't want anyone to see me like this, least of all Holly. My lips are swollen, my panties are soaked, and my heart? It's pounding so loudly, I'm surprised no one can hear it but me. My throat aches with emotion, and I squeeze my eyes closed and command my shaking body to focus on breathing. *In through the nose, out through the mouth.*

But as soon as I close my eyes, I can feel Hayes's lips on mine. Warm and insistent, pushing and pulling against my mouth with a passion I've never experienced before, until suddenly his lips were gone. Until I took things too far and he asked me to leave. Talk about embarrassing.

A hot shiver creeps over my skin. God, what did I expect? That after twenty years of treating me like a little sister, Hayes would suddenly see me as some sexpot and take me to bed? Life just doesn't work that way. Not for me, anyway. Years of watching Hayes leave parties with different girls, and then later, leaving bars with different women, should have cemented that into my brain.

I'm not his type. Period. End of story.

I don't want to face Holly right now, but what choice do I have? I'm just considering sneaking to the kitchen for something strong and potent to drink away my shame when the door to Hayes's room opens, and his deep voice rumbles out my name.

"Maren."

Hope blooms in my chest, curling inside me, sliding lower. I take another deep breath to steady myself. *God, I ache for him.*

When I turn to face him, his eyes are dark and conflicted. The promise of hot sex and power radiates from him in waves. He tilts his head, still waiting. I have no idea what to say.

I drop my gaze, unable to meet his eyes. I can't take more of his rejection, especially not now, here in the light of the hallway where I have to watch his dark gaze moving over my exposed skin. Where I can feel the desire radiating between us.

He's infuriating. And intoxicating.

Finally, my eyes meet his, and heat bolts through me.

He steps closer, his fingers press beneath my chin, and he lifts my face toward his. His sensual mouth presses into a firm line, and my stomach squeezes.

"Come back to my room." It's less of a request than it is a demand, and I can't tame the hot desire that twists through me once again. "Please," he adds, his voice tight.

When I dare to meet his gaze again, his eyes have softened. They remind me of rye whiskey, which is oddly relevant to my escape plan to drink myself to sleep. It's the only way to quiet this ache.

"We don't need to have this conversation. You made yourself clear," I choke out, saddened by how pathetic and broken I sound. A single tear slips down my cheek, threatening to turn into a full-on breakdown. "I'm sorry, okay? I really am. It's my fault."

"No, no, dove," he murmurs, wiping the tear from my cheek with his thumb. "Believe me, pushing you away was the hardest thing I've ever done."

Is he patronizing me? He seems so sincere, but pity can be sincere. Very much so.

I take a shaky breath, checking over my shoulder. This scene would be suspicious to anyone getting out of bed for a bathroom trip or a glass of water. Wolfie could walk down this hall at any—

"Maren."

Hayes's fingers brush through my mussed hair, tucking unruly strands behind my ear before he leans in, his lips brushing against my ear in a whisper. "Please, dove. Come back to bed with me."

And just like that, I melt, my body responding again.

His hand sneaks around the back of my neck, massaging the tense muscles there as he leads me back inside his room. When the door closes, we stand in the dark, connected only by his fingers trailing through my hair.

It feels so good, I can barely breathe . . . and hardly dare hope for what might happen next.

"I'll turn on the light," he finally mumbles, releasing me and walking back to the bed. He sits on the edge, leaning over to turn on the lamp, which casts dim yellow light over his features.

In the hallway, I didn't register how disheveled he looks. His hair is messy, hands clenched, a pair of gray boxers hanging low on his hips. His blush can't compare to mine, but there's still a distinct coloring across his cheekbones.

I carefully make my way to the opposite corner of the bed and sit. Hayes shifts so that he's looking directly at me. How can he be so confident still?

"What was going through your head? When you kissed me?" he asks, dropping his gaze to the stretch of wrinkled sheets between us.

What a question. It almost knocks the breath from my lungs.

"I don't know. I guess I . . . I've always wondered, you know? What did those other girls have that I don't." Saying it out loud is like taking bolt cutters to the padlocks on my heart. I'm worried what else will slip out of the vault.

"Nothing. They had nothing on you, dove."

I scoff. Now I know for sure he's patronizing me.

"Be real," I say, shooting him a skeptical look while my fingers busy themselves along the hem of my T-shirt.

"I am."

From the look on his face, the same face I've known nearly my whole life . . . he's not lying. My heart skips a beat.

"My turn," I say, my throat tight. "Today in the water, I felt you . . ." I pause and look down, then meet his eyes again when I find my courage. "I felt you get hard. Was that real?"

Hayes closes his eyes for a moment, his brows furrowing together in some sort of inner turmoil. When he opens his eyes again, he almost looks sad. "Real. Very real," he says, his voice softer than I've ever heard it before.

He looks so vulnerable right now, so different from the powerhouse of a man I've come to know and admire. Is he only trying to be gentle with me? Because the vulnerable expression on his face is doing things for me that I'd rather not say out loud.

I want you so much.

Slowly, I lean over the bed, crawling toward him. The closer I get, the more the apprehension in his eyes melts into what I can only describe as lust.

Does he want me too?

I only stop when we're a breath apart. Still on my knees, I reach with one finger to trace his sharp, clenched jawline. Hayes's dark, dilated eyes are fixed on my lips now. With my finger, I trace the outline of his plump bottom lip. The unasked question floats in the air between us.

And when I kiss him again, I know I won't be able to stop.

Hayes sighs into my mouth, his big, strong hands reaching up to cup my face before pushing into my hair. His lips move against mine urgently, his hot tongue sliding inside, flicking against mine with a delicious slickness. With a handful of my hair gripped firmly, but not painfully, he angles our kisses deeper than before. I can't contain the moan that escapes my throat.

When I gasp for air, Hayes runs his hot mouth against my jaw, my neck, my still-clothed shoulder. I raise my arms, and he takes the hint, lifting the oversized T-shirt over my head. When his gaze lowers to my bare breasts, I suck in a breath, and when his palms brush the tender skin along their sides, my nipples go erect.

"So fucking perfect," he rasps into my ear, lightly pinching one nipple.

I nearly jolt. *Shit*. It's been a long time since a man has touched me. And this is *Hayes*.

Everything feels electrified. The heavy thump of my heart. His big hands holding mine. But it's his eyes that dismantle me. Long, impossibly thick lashes. So much hot emotion reflected back at me.

So many times, I've imagined the kind of lover Hayes would be. Demanding. In control. Generous.

"Lay down," he whispers, and I obey without a thought.

His muscled body stretches over mine, enveloping me in his warmth and his weight. He supports himself on his forearms, and I spread my legs for him, lifting my hips to brush myself against his abdomen. When his rock-hard erection rubs against my core, I gasp with surprise. It's longer, thicker, and hotter than I remember from the lake.

Tracing my fingers along the defined lines of his pecs, abs, and obliques, I'm dizzy with desire. When he pushes his length against the front of my damp panties, he does so with slow, deliberate strokes. I claw at his hips, my head spinning with attraction. I've never wanted anyone more, and try to push his boxers down with my feet, but he moves away.

Hayes kisses a trail down my neck to my

breasts, his tongue flicking out to brush against one peaked nipple. I cry out, my back arching in ecstasy as he wraps his lips around the taut, sensitive flesh, sucking, nipping, and licking away like my tit is his favorite flavor of ice cream. I tangle my fingers in his hair, pulling tight when I feel his fingertips exploring the skin of my thighs, the edge of my panties. Without removing the wet cotton, Hayes finds my most sensitive spot and gives it a gentle tap.

I groan, covering my mouth with one hand to muffle the sound.

He chuckles against my breast, his head dipping lower to kiss the exposed skin of my belly. His fingers dance around my cotton-clad core, stopping only to rub my clit in precise, even circles. I'm already unravelling by the time Hayes hooks his fingers around my panties, pulling them down the length of my legs. With two hands, he spreads my knees, looking down at the bare spot between my legs for the very first time.

"Dove," he says softly, running one hand up and down my thigh.

I shiver at his touch, gripping the sheets around me. I've never been this exposed before, never even imagined it. But with Hayes's eyes on me, I feel alive.

Suddenly, he's kissing a line down my thigh toward my center, pausing to tease me with hot strokes of his wet, talented tongue.

"You—*ahhh*—you don't have to—" I stammer between pants.

Wrapping one arm around my thigh and cupping one ass cheek with the other hand, Hayes looks up from between my legs, his eyes flashing. "I want to. You don't know how long," he says, pausing to press another kiss to my most sensitive spot, "I've wanted to . . ."

I arch my back yet again, giving in to the mind-numbing pleasure of Hayes doing something he very clearly excels at. My toes flex and twitch as he massages my buttock with one hand, his tongue circling my clit.

It goes on like this for a while, Hayes licking my pussy with sloppy, wet kisses, and me grinding myself against his greedy mouth. Just when I feel like I can't take it any longer, I feel one of Hayes's long fingers tracing my flesh.

His lips latch onto my clit, sucking hard as his finger dips inside me, curling at just the right spot. I can feel my orgasm crashing toward me, lost in the sensations of pleasure so intense, I don't remember anything ever feeling like this. When he slips another finger inside me, I lose it, biting down on my fist to hush the animalistic moan that escapes me as I come harder, faster, and longer than I ever have before.

When I come back down to earth, my body is covered in sweat, my breasts heaving with the effort it's taking me to catch my breath. Hayes is still pressing gentle kisses to my core, sending jolts of pleasure through me with each contact. Half of me could just float away on the waves of this blissful existence forever, but another, more insistent half would prefer to return the favor.

"How do you feel?" he asks, his voice low and sweet. His lips tickle the bare skin of my thigh.

"I feel . . . like we're not done here."

He raises one brow in question as I swing my legs over the side of the bed, a newfound energy bubbling inside me. When my knees touch the floor, Hayes's expression comically shifts from wonder to sheer lust.

Positioning myself between his parted knees, I rub one hand over the erect length of him through his boxers, enjoying how he twitches beneath my touch. A rough breath escapes his parted lips as I grip the elastic, giving the fabric a soft pull.

The cotton gives way and I inhale, suddenly

speechless.

His penis is huge. Hard. Daunting. But the desire I have to touch it, suck it—*ride* it—is an urgent need.

But before I can finish unwrapping my present, Hayes catches my hands and stops me.

Eleven

HAYES

As I gaze down at Maren kneeling in front of me, my heart pounds in anticipation. God, she's perfect. Petite and curvy and so luscious, I want to devour her all over again.

I know I should stop her from doing this, but I can't.

When I release her hands, she gives me a small smirk. Her full breasts still heave with her breathlessness, and I want to bury my face between them and kiss and suck. But all I can do is sit here on the edge of the bed like a statue and watch as she lowers her mouth to my cock.

With tentative flicks of her hot tongue, she teases me at first. I bury my fists into the blankets as she opens wider and works to fit the head of my cock into her perfect mouth.

"*Fuck.* Yeah, that's it." I lift my hips from the mattress, giving her more.

Maren makes a breathless sound, her tongue teasing as she takes a much-needed gulp of oxygen. She cups my balls in one hand and strokes my aching shaft with the other. Her eyes sink closed as she takes me in her mouth again.

"Dove . . ." I rasp out the word, already breathless.

I'm going to hell. That much is obvious. Because Maren is treating me to a hot, wet blow job, and it's the closest I've ever been to heaven.

I touch her hair, placing my thumb on the side of her throat to feel her accepting me, and Maren lets out a helpless little whimper. I can't help but talk dirty to her, tell her how sexy she looks with her mouth full of my cock, how good she is at this. And I savor each of her reactions. The way she murmurs against me and squeezes her thighs together . . . it's hot as hell.

Before I come, I warn her, but Maren doesn't stop, forcing even more of me into her throat just as I explode.

"Hell, sweetheart." I gasp as she sits back on her heels, looking pleased. Who would have known that *that* was one of Maren's many talents? Not this guy.

Pulling her up onto the bed and against my chest afterward is the most natural thing in the world. She lets out a small giggle and lays her head on my shoulder. Lying here with her, cuddled together in a warm, flushed heap, feels almost as good as the intimacy we just shared. This is all so unexpected, but at the same time, it feels right.

As I hold her close and gently run my knuckles over the smooth skin of her spine, I try to convince myself that maybe my betrayal of Wolfie's trust doesn't count across state lines.

It almost works.

We cuddle until I fall asleep. At some point, Maren must have slipped out of bed. The next morning, I wake alone and full of guilt.

What the fuck happened last night? Did I let things go too far? I've almost convinced myself that it was all just a wet dream, until I come downstairs for breakfast and find Maren and Wolfie sitting at the table, the smell of coffee hanging heavy in the air.

Wolfie is glued to his phone, his hair sticking

out at odd angles, his face screwed up in a scowl. We all know better than to talk to him before his third cup. Maren brings her mug to her lips and looks at me over the thin wisp of steam.

"Morning, Hayes. Sleep well?" Her voice is like velvet, her lids heavy as she sips her coffee without taking her gaze from mine.

All right. Definitely not a dream.

It's a good thing Wolfie is dead to the world right now, because it doesn't take a psychic to interpret the vibes between us.

"Uh . . . yeah," I manage to say before I tear my gaze away from her and pour myself some coffee.

I'm fucked. We're fucked. I'm so going to hell. And it doesn't help that just being in the same room as Maren is turning me on.

One by one, the rest of the crew join us in the kitchen.

Connor bounds down the stairs, slapping Wolfie on the shoulder with a loud, "Good morning!" Wolfie growls in response. Penelope and Scarlett arrive together and sit by Maren at the table, and Caleb starts cracking eggs into a bowl.

Finally, Holly saunters down the stairs, the only one of us already dressed in a swimsuit and a lacy cover-up that looks more like lingerie than sleep-wear. After last night, I'm about ready to slaughter Wolfie for inviting her.

"Good morning, everyone," she says in a sing-song voice, flouncing around the kitchen island. "Sleep well? I certainly did. Maren, I hope I didn't disturb you last night. I've been known to toss and turn and make a lot of noise in the night." She curls a lock of her dark hair around her finger and bats her lashes apologetically Maren's way.

With every second I spend around this woman, it's getting harder and harder to believe I was ever attracted to her.

Maren glances at me, and her eyes tell me everything I need to know. She's thinking of last night. Of how Holly's little show drove us into the same room. Of what happened after . . . how I tasted her, made her moan and twitch with my tongue, how she took every last drop of me down her throat.

Fuck. I've got to get a hold of myself.

I look away and busy my hands by making an-other pot of coffee and trying to think of literally anything else. Connor and Caleb are chatting about our plans for the morning out on the water, so I nod along with their conversation and pretend I'm paying attention. But really, I'm listening to Maren, who's coolly telling Holly that she didn't disturb her at all, and that she slept in perfect bliss. I don't have to see the look on Holly's face to know that's not the answer she was hoping for.

After breakfast, we all change into our suits and meet out on the dock. Caleb, Connor, and Wolfie haul a few kayaks into the water and try to persuade the girls to get in with them. I grab a couple of paddleboards from the rack and nod to Maren.

"Is your balance still as good as it was in high school?" I ask, holding a paddle out to her.

She smiles and opens her mouth to answer, but Wolfie's voice cuts her off.

"Hayes! Would you get your ass over here and explain to Penelope that these kayaks are designed for two people?"

I sigh and drop the boards. "Be right back."

Maren shrugs in understanding, and I make my way to the water, where something I can't quite figure out is going on between Wolfie and Penelope. Are they . . . flirting?

"I'm not getting in that thing with you, Wolfie!" she squeals, slapping his arm with the back of her hand.

Wolfie's mouth twists into a sideways grin.

What the hell? Looks like I'm not the only one thinking things they shouldn't these days.

"What seems to be the problem here, folks?" I ask, clasping my hands together and giving Wolfie an easy smile.

Penelope crosses her arms, and Wolfie holds his out by his sides.

"I thought it'd be nice for the two of us to take a little trip around the lake, but Pen doesn't seem so sure," he says, his usual growl less angry and more playful than usual.

"I just don't think it's safe," Penelope says, looking worriedly at the kayak.

"We take these bad boys out on the water all the time. If they weren't safe, we wouldn't have them," I tell her with a reassuring nod.

"Well, if they're so safe, you two can take it. I'm going to go paddleboard with Maren," Penelope says, tossing her hair over her shoulder and leaving in a huff.

Wolfie grunts and watches her leave, a dumbfounded look on his face.

"Smooth, bro," I say, giving his arm a good-natured punch. *Now both our plans for the day are ruined.*

"Shut up."

We spend the morning on the water, kayaking, paddleboarding, floating around in inner tubes, doing pretty much whatever activity we can get our hands on. Later that afternoon, we pack up and pile into the cars to head back into the city, worn out and a little sunburned from our weekend away.

In the car, Wolfie turns the radio to the same station as always. He drums his fingers on the steering wheel along to some classic rock, and I do my best to avoid staring at Maren's reflection in the rearview mirror every chance I get.

She's quiet, and that's not like her. My plan to steal a few moments alone on the water was ruined by Penelope, so I have no idea where Maren's head is at. I can only imagine what she must think of me now—her older brother's best friend who took advantage of her when she was in a vulnerable situation. I never should have invited her into my bed last night. It was a mistake, and I'll apologize the first chance I get.

Or maybe that's not the case. Maybe she's qui-

et because she's planning how to tell Wolfie. Or
. . . maybe she's planning when we'll do it again.
Either way, I have to know what she's thinking. I
need to talk to her and make sure she's okay.

My place is on the way to each of theirs, so
Wolfie drops me off first. Outside my apartment,
he salutes me from the driver's side while Maren
smiles from the passenger seat.

"Thanks again for a fun weekend, Hayes. It was
really sweet of you to have us all over," she says.

"Anytime."

"See you bright and early tomorrow," Wolfie
says and rolls up the window before driving away.

I trudge myself and my duffel upstairs, wishing
Maren had given me some kind of code to crack
instead of a polite, generic thank-you. I still have
no idea what she's thinking, but I know now what
I have to do.

Wolfie will be dropping off Maren next. Her
place isn't far from mine, so I'd say I have a good
ten minutes before she's alone in her apartment. I
catch up with Rosie for a few minutes, starting to
fill her in on the weekend. When the time comes,
I excuse myself to my bedroom and dial Maren's
number, unconsciously holding my breath while it
rings.

"Did you forget something?" Maren's tone is teasing, playful. Too playful for her to still be with Wolfie.

"Are you alone?"

"He just dropped me off."

"I just, I wanted to make sure that you're okay."

She doesn't respond right away, and I can hear her keys jangling and the door closing behind her.

"Are you okay?" I repeat.

"What are you asking me, Hayes?"

"I mean, did we—did I—I wanted to make sure I didn't cross a line last night."

She giggles, but not the light, airy, girlish giggle I'm used to. This one comes from somewhere deep in her throat, somewhere sensual.

"Of course I'm okay." She laughs a little, and it sounds like she wants to say something else, but she doesn't.

I let out a relieved breath. "Good. I'm glad to hear that."

She giggles again. "You know, I'm glad you called, actually. I have something I wanted to talk to you about."

"Oh?"

"I was wondering if you wanted to come to the fundraiser with me next weekend."

"Like as your date?"

"No. I don't know. I just figured since you were so important and instrumental in making it all happen, it'd be nice to have you there with us. But I totally understand if you—"

"I'll be there."

"Really?"

"Of course. I wouldn't miss it for the world."

We chat a little while longer about a few final details for the fundraiser before hanging up. When I walk out into the kitchen for a glass of water, I find Rosie sitting at the table, painting her fingernails a bright shade of pink.

"You look like hell," she says, glancing up at me over her glasses.

"I missed you too."

"What's wrong? Did something happen at the lake house? You know, sometimes too much sun can make people do things they don't mean."

If you only knew.

I take a sip of water, the liquid cool going down my throat. "I'm fine. Nothing happened. We all had a good time."

She narrows her eyes. "Well, make sure you drink two of those. You're probably sunburned under that shirt. No one applies sunscreen properly these days."

I nod and refill my glass. "I'm exhausted. I'll see you in the morning, okay? Love you."

"I love you too."

I trudge back to my room and shut the door behind me.

That phone call with Maren should have made me feel better, so why do I feel like a piece of shit that's just been run over by a dump truck? She might not think we crossed a line, but I'm starting to wonder if we're both in the wrong here. I might want her, and she might want me, but that doesn't make what we did right.

Later, I fall asleep, huddled alone under the blankets. Just like I do every night.

Twelve

MAREN

The morning of the fundraiser, I wake up with butterflies in my belly. It's half excitement, half nervous energy, and my stomach churns because I need tonight to go well.

I reflexively reach for my phone, scrolling through my social media feed in an effort to quiet my mind. Immediately, I land on a photo of Wolfie and Hayes at the beach last weekend, drenched in lake water and sunlight. My brother, ever the stoic one, is frowning. But the huge, genuine smile on Hayes's face makes my heart swell with emotion.

What happened at the lake house was . . . surreal. Ever since, I've spent every night tossing and turning between vivid memories and hazy dreams of Hayes's lips on my skin, his tongue tracing sensual lines down my body, worshipping my most sensitive spots. When I close my eyes, I can still hear his moan as I fondled his length before coating it with hot, wet kisses.

Are you okay?

When he asked me that question so sincerely, I wanted to blurt, *I'm better than okay.* But we're exploring entirely new territory now, terrain left untouched during years of platonic friendship and stolen glances. I have to curb my enthusiasm if I want to stay on Hayes's radar as more than his best friend's sister. But I'm not *too* worried . . . after all, I have a lot of practice at it.

I open my messages and begin drafting a text to Hayes before I can psych myself out.

Ready for tonight?

Though I'm tempted to sit on my bed and wait for his response, I toss my phone back on the duvet and head for the bathroom.

The hot water from the shower eases the stress in my shoulders and neck, a small relief that I don't take for granted. Lathering up some shaving cream in my hands, I cover my legs one by one. I love the repetitive action of drawing a razor ever so gently over my skin. When I'm cleaning up my bikini line, the memory of Hayes's eyes flashing up to mine from between my legs sends a shock straight to my core.

I let the water turn cold before I get out of the shower, a rush of reality to remind me of my first priority—making nice with the rich friends of Riverside tonight. *Not* having life-altering sex with Hayes Ellison.

When I return to my room wrapped in a damp towel, a *buzz-buzz* draws me back to my bed.

I'll pick you up at seven.

His message is short and to the point. It does nothing to ease the anxiety stewing inside me.

Sitting in Hayes's Lexus that evening, I periodically check my phone to make sure the venue hasn't burned to the ground or the caterers haven't forgotten the vegan options.

Since the fundraiser was my brainchild, Peggy insisted that I leave all the extra event prep to her and her team of student volunteers. When I called her just hours ago to suggest I could arrive early to coordinate the auction arrangements, she stopped me cold.

"No, no, no, enough of that. We'll take care of the setup. You take your time. Arrive in style!"

This is about as stylish as I get, but it's certainly not an outfit to be ignored. The fancy dresses in the back of my closet were looking a little worn from too many semi-formals and weddings, so I turned to my good friend the internet for some consignment designer options.

My tanned legs peek out of the long slit along the side of the creamy silk gown. The gold accents around the bodice frame my neck and breasts perfectly, neither too subtle nor too gaudy. My long brown hair is pulled to the side, a waterfall of curls secured over one shoulder with an elegant clip my grandmother once gave me. My makeup is all natural except for a matte-nutmeg lipstick I bought on a whim during a downtown shopping spree. It may have taken three hours to get ready for tonight, but I look good.

And my date, well, he looks like he belongs on the cover of *GQ* magazine, his hair slicked back into a natural wave, and his well-tailored tuxedo accentuating those broad, sexy shoulders. When Hayes's impossibly sharp eyes meet mine, I have to remind my lungs to keep breathing.

"What's the game plan for tonight?" he asks, glancing between me and the road. "You're courting some pretty big money, so does that make me your wingman?"

"That's the idea," I say, pulling a binder from the very unstylish tote bag I plan to leave in the car. "I've memorized every guest's name, vocation, and relationship to Riverside, but if you want to take a look before we go in, there should be time."

Eyeing the binder, Hayes chuckles. "I trust you. We've still got another forty minutes to go, so give me the SparkNotes version."

"Sure."

After a half hour of my describing each guest, from most influential to least, Hayes reaches over and closes the binder with a firm hand.

"You're killing me," he says with a groan. "I can't hear about one more philanthropic entrepreneur who prefers the White Sox to the Cubs. How the hell did you find time to put all of this together?"

"A few late nights," I say with a shrug. "It's all online if you know where to look."

He sighs, sounding bored already. "I bet."

I reach over to place a hand on his forearm.

"This is going to be fun, okay? I don't know about you, but I'm certainly having a glass of champagne."

"Or twelve," he mutters with a smirk.

"Or twelve. You can drink as much as you'd like. Just in case, I reserved a hotel room at the venue, in the event we don't want to risk the drive home."

The air between us is suddenly charged, my fingertips on his jacket sleeve electrified. Neither of us has dared mention again what happened at the lake house, but I can feel our attraction in every heated look, in every tension-filled stare.

Hayes finally grunts, his eyes fixed on the road ahead. "Probably a good idea."

I breathe out a soft sigh of relief.

Reserving only one hotel room was a big move on my part, but he doesn't seem upset or uncomfortable. Truthfully, my bank account would never recover from a purchase of two reservations this close to when rent's due. Also truthfully, the idea of sharing a room with Hayes after a fancy night like this really excites me. More than it probably should.

When we arrive, Hayes and I stride past the coat

check and a gathering of young volunteers, straight through the double doors. The view is astonishing.

The vaulted ceiling is dripping with tiny Edison bulbs, casting a deep glow upon all the arriving guests. Tall cabaret tables are decorated with simple, but eye-catching floral centerpieces. On the far side of the room sits an expansive table where the buffet will take place, all the catered food warming over wick fuel cans. Situated around the perimeter of the room are displays of the auction items—coveted Chicago memorabilia and collectibles, and experience packages from popular massage studios, luxury cruise lines, and prominent theater companies.

I must be gawking because Hayes puts his warm palm against the small of my back and gently urges me forward.

"Let's get to work, shall we?" he whispers in my ear.

When my wide eyes meet his confident gaze, his sensual mouth slides into a relaxed smile. Straightening his shoulders, he hooks my arm into the crook of his elbow. My skin lights up like fireworks at his touch, waking me up from my stupor.

I nod toward an older man peering over a nearby display case and whisper his name into my date's ear. I feel more confident in heels, so I can easily keep up with Hayes's long strides as we approach the gentleman.

Before we reach our target, I catch Peggy's eye from across the room where she's entertaining a circle of familiar guests. She looks absolutely lovely in her floor-length purple gown. She gives me an enthusiastic thumbs-up, and before long, half the room's eyes are on me. Not only on me . . . *on Hayes*. It occurs to me that I probably have the most handsome date in the room.

I squeeze his arm tightly as we approach Gene Westwood, CEO of one of the city's most well-respected investment firms, known for its involvement in various philanthropic efforts.

"Gene?"

He turns around with a look of interest, his white eyebrows raised. "Yes?"

"My name is Maren. We spoke on the phone earlier this week. It's so lovely to meet you in person," I say as I extend one hand.

Gene accepts with a hearty shake, a wide smile stretching across his kindly, aged face. "Excellent. So nice to meet you. And this is your husband?"

My heart leaps into my throat but I recover immediately, masking my blush with a smile. "No, Hayes is . . . the inspiration behind the evening. And a very close friend of mine."

The man on my arm shoots me a sly look that says—*Inspiration, huh?*—before outstretching his own hand toward Gene, who accepts it with another firm handshake.

"Happy to meet you. Are you enjoying yourself?" Hayes asks, exuding confidence and hospitality.

God, he's sexy like this.

"Why, yes. What a fantastic event you've both put together," Gene says, gesturing toward the auction items.

"Thank you," I say, almost positive now that I can convince him to bid generously. With a grateful look around the room, I murmur, "We've been very lucky. Everyone has been so compassionate."

"Now, now, don't let anyone take the credit for your hard work," Gene says, leaning in to give me a secretive wink. "My wife and I were just talking about bidding on this World Series treasure you've landed. She's a bigger baseball fan than even me, so you can consider us sold."

"That's wonderful to hear." Honestly, I'm just

relieved that the subject came up so naturally.

"That jersey in particular will become a sought-after collector's item in fifteen, twenty years," Hayes says, waving Gene over to look more closely at the worn fabric. "The patch on the sleeve is what makes it priceless. It belongs in the hands of someone who will truly cherish it."

"Indeed it does," Gene mutters, nodding enthusiastically.

Seeing the excitement in his eyes, I reach over to squeeze Hayes's hand. *Thank you.*

The night continues like this, with the two of us making casual but purposeful conversation with some of the biggest moguls in Chicago, only pausing to fill our plates with food from the buffet.

When the band on the corner stage starts playing some soft, crooning jazz, Hayes extends his hand to me. "May I have this dance?"

"Absolutely," I say, taming my grin into a casual smile.

I slip my hand into his and follow his lead to the dance floor, a slightly upraised stretch of shiny, polished mahogany. Hayes stops, one hand sliding down my arm to lift my hand into his strong, sure grasp, and the other wandering around to the small of my back.

I allow myself to be tucked into his swaying embrace, resting my temple against his shoulder. He smells sweet and earthy, like a spring morning after a full night of rain. Closing my eyes, I sigh deeply, the stress of Riverside's fate loosening its claws around my heart.

"We make quite the money magnet, don't we?" Hayes says, his voice rumbling against my hair. His fingers trace shapes along the silk of my dress, scorching the skin beneath with hot excitement.

"It helps that you have the charisma to carry the conversation," I say with a chuckle. "I can't improvise like that. Just the thought of it gives me hives."

Hayes snorts. "My charisma wouldn't do shit without your earnestness. You're very easy to fall for."

I lean back to look him sternly in the eye, which proves to be a mistake. Making eye contact with Hayes is like diving headfirst into a vat of the sweetest, stickiest honey. *Good luck getting out.*

"That sounds like a charmed existence," I say, looking up at him through my eyelashes. "What do you think? Should I quit my job to become someone's sordid mistress?"

"I'd laugh, but let's be real. You'd never leave Riverside."

Surprised, I blink. "Why do you say that?"

"You did all of this. You spent the last month working your ass off to, what, quit and move on to something else?" he murmurs, releasing my hand to cup my cheek. Our feet stop moving, our eyes dancing as we gaze at each other. "That's why you're special. Work has never been about money to you. It's always been about how much you care, dove."

When I'm speechless, Hayes smirks and goes back to swaying with me in his arms.

How is it that every time I try to have a light, casual moment with Hayes, it always turns into *this*? This smoldering, heart-on-fire, can't-catch-a-breath feeling?

"You know me pretty well, don't you, Hayes Ellison?" I whisper, searching his eyes for some sort of sign, some clue that I'm not imagining this all-consuming fire between us.

"I pay attention, Maren Cox." His thumb caresses my cheek, his eyes fixed on my lips.

Please kiss me. Please kiss me.

"Hayes—"

"Maren!" calls a female voice from behind me.

I swallow my words, turning around to see Peggy waddling toward us, waving a legal pad in the air.

"Maren," she says, panting, "I've been looking for you."

"What's wrong?" I ask, trying my best to ignore the sensation of my date's fingers, still pressed against the silk of my gown.

"Nothing is wrong." She beams, her teary eyes threatening to spill onto her rouged cheeks. "I've just tallied up the final list. It's a miracle. Look!"

The paper she's showing me is the list of highest bidders. I follow her finger down the length of the page, landing on the final auction item: 2016 World Series Cubs v. Indians Memorabilia. A familiar name is scrawled next to a number with far more zeros than I think I've ever seen outside of an episode of *Mad Men*.

"Gene and Miriam Westwood . . . sixty *thousand* dollars?" I gasp, the music and chattering of the room only white noise to the beat of my hammering heart.

"I was wondering if you'd like to do the honors of rewarding the highest bidders, my dear," Peggy says, reaching out to squeeze my hand. "You deserve it. The stage is yours."

Glancing back at Hayes and his encouraging eyes is enough to solidify the truth I've been praying for. *Riverside is saved.*

"I would love nothing more."

After the last guests have said their good-byes and left for the evening, Hayes and I stick around to clean up whatever we can.

I'm on garbage patrol, limping around with sore feet and a giant garbage bag, tossing the debris of the evening inside. Hayes, meanwhile, helps a handful of volunteers disassemble the stage and carry the tables to the storage closet. He stripped off his tuxedo jacket when we began to help, and it's impossible not to stare at that muscled back. A low tingle in my belly reminds me what else the night has in store for me.

We stop by the car to pick up my tote bag, which contains pajamas for me, my toothbrush, and an extra I picked up for Hayes earlier this week. Leaning against the car in the cool night air, I toss my creepy donor-stalking binder into the back seat. When I reach for the bag again, Hayes intercepts me.

"I've got it."

"You know, you don't have to do the whole gentleman act still," I say before leaning in to whisper, "I think the fancy part of the evening is over."

"Oh, in that case—"

Hayes swings my bag around and around, threatening to dump all of its contents onto the parking lot.

"No, Hayes!" I laugh, reaching for him. "Okay, okay, five more minutes of gentlemanly behavior, and then you're free to be a savage."

Hayes sighs dramatically, muttering that five minutes is too long. He straightens his shoulders, threading one arm through the loops of my bag before offering me the other to lean on. Smirking, I wrap my hand around his firm bicep and shuffle alongside him toward the hotel.

It only takes minutes to sign in and get our room key. In the elevator, I lean against the wall, a small smile on my lips at how well tonight's event went. Hayes leans against the opposite wall, watching me.

"How do you feel?" he asks, his voice so tender it should be illegal.

"Exhausted." I sigh, cocking my head to the side to give him a tired smile. "Happy. Free."

"Free?"

"It's like a weight has been lifted off my shoulders," I murmur, closing my eyes. "It's like I've been underwater this whole month, and now I can finally breathe again."

When I open my eyes, Hayes is looking at his wristwatch.

"I'm sorry," I say with a huff. "Am I boring you?"

"Not at all." He smirks, but his eyes stay locked on the silver accessory.

"Then what are you waiting for?" I ask, rolling my eyes.

He holds up one finger, an annoying gesture to wait. Finally, he drops his arms, my bag, and its contents along with them.

"Seriously, Hayes? What's wrong with y—"

With one long stride, he's on me, his hands on my jaw, angling my mouth up to his in a kiss so fiery, it sears right through me. All questions die on my lips as the kiss overwhelms me.

I clutch his shoulders with desperate fingers,

my mind deliciously blank. Greedy for more, I open my mouth to his insistent tongue, which eagerly slips inside to caress my own. One long leg presses between mine and rubs against my core with a satisfying urgency. When he releases me, our lips parting, his eyes are nearly black with desire.

"What was that for?" I ask, breathless.

Hayes leans in, tracing a path down my neck with his hot, wet tongue. "Your five minutes are up. Time to be a savage."

Thirteen

HAYES

The door slams shut behind us, and I press Maren against it.

It's like the tension that's been building all night has finally burst, and we're helpless against it. *I'm* helpless against it. I've wanted this for so long, and the moment her mouth met mine in the elevator, I knew she wanted this too. So to be here now, to know what's coming next, it's almost too much to handle.

Almost.

I bring my hands to her hips and drag her body closer so we're pressed tightly together. She lets out a little sound of surprise when she feels how hard I am. And believe me, I'm hard enough to pound nails.

Fuck. Slow down, Hayes.

I press my forehead to hers and draw a breath, my voice raspy as I say, "Dove."

She touches my jaw, tilting my mouth back down to hers. "More."

I groan and give in, kissing her deeply. My tongue tangles with hers, and I feel powerless to do anything but give her everything she wants. And it's obvious she wants *this*—more kissing and less talking.

Her hands reach for my jacket, and she peels away the first layer of clothing between us. I reach for her hair, cradling the back of her head as I slide my tongue into her mouth. She moans and bucks her hips into me, clearly telegraphing her thoughts. *Less clothes. Now.*

I guide us to the king-size bed, removing my shirt in the process. Maren unzips her dress and begins to pull it over her head, but I stop her, holding her hands by her wrists.

"Let me."

She nods, and I lift her arms over her head before bending down to gather the hem of her skirt. Slowly and with pleasure, I peel the dress from her body, kissing each new portion of skin I reveal along the way. Her knees, her thighs, her hips, her belly. When I reach her mouth, I drop the dress to the floor, and we fall onto the bed together.

"You're so beautiful," I say softly, taking her breast in my hand and rolling her nipple between my fingers, and she sighs and throws her head back.

I want to savor every moment of our first time together. I want us to enjoy this. I want *her* to enjoy this. I want her to be ready.

"Come here," I say, and Maren obeys, climbing on top of me so that my cock strains behind my zipper, pressing into her center. "Ride me."

She looks at me for a moment, her eyes full of lust and hunger and a hint of confusion. I grind up into her. She shudders and smiles in understanding. With one hand splayed against my abs, she gyrates her hips over mine, moans instantly pouring from her lips. It only makes me harder to see her like this, using me for her pleasure, getting herself off.

I pull her face down to mine and kiss her again, deeper and more urgently than before, moving my hips against her rhythm. She sighs into my mouth, and when she pulls away panting, her face is flushed, her hair spilling over one shoulder. God, she's beautiful like this.

"I need you," she says, panting out the words

between breaths.

She climbs off me only long enough to shimmy out of her panties. I draw down the zipper to my dress pants, and Maren tugs them down my hips.

I could almost laugh at how eager she is. But right now, there's no humor. Just a whole lot of sexual tension—tension that's been building for actual *years*.

I'm so desperate for her, I could burst. But I vow not to, not until she's come for me first. I pull off my boxer briefs and drop them over the side of the bed. Maren's eyes drink me in, widening slightly as they settle for a moment at my crotch.

I press my lips to her neck as she climbs back on top of me. This time, I feel how wet she is, and I groan as she moves her hips and we slide together.

Clutching her hip in one hand, I slow her movements.

"Could you come like this?" she asks, a mischievous smile tilting her lips.

Could I come like this? She really has no idea what she does to me. "Is that what you want?"

She bites her bottom lip and shakes her head. "I want you inside me."

"Condom?" I ask softly.

She meets my eyes. "I'm good if you are."

"I'm . . . good," I say, breathing out the word. I've always used condoms. Always. But Maren is different. And since I haven't been with anyone since Samantha dumped me, and I was tested right after that, I know I won't be putting Maren at risk.

Lifting up on her knees, she brings one hand between us to lift my cock from my stomach and then . . . *fuuck.*

Breathe, Hayes.

She's hot and tight and so perfect.

I groan at the amazing warmth that greets me. She lowers herself, sliding slowly as she adjusts to the feel of me stretching her.

Her eyes sink closed and she makes a low, pleasure-filled sound. *"Hayes."*

"Fuck, you feel so good." I growl out the words, rising up on my elbows to nip at the soft spot between her ear and shoulder.

She gasps as I thrust deeper into her, every inch a step closer to heaven. She takes me until I'm fully inside her, and every muscle in my body tightens to avoid the pending orgasm I can feel building at the base of my spine.

It doesn't take long for her to find her rhythm. The sounds coming out of her mouth are other-worldly.

Maren's the best thing I've ever felt, and that knowledge doesn't settle well with me. It's a dangerous realization that I don't have time to dwell on because she begins moving faster, her cries growing louder.

As she comes apart, it's the most beautiful thing I've ever witnessed. Her cheeks are flushed, her lips swollen, and her hair is wild. I wish I could slow time, wish I could focus on each little detail of this moment, but Maren's beginning to unravel, and I know I won't be far behind. When she finishes, I clutch her tightly, erupting with a wild bolt of pleasure that I feel through every nerve ending. After, we collapse back onto the bed together, our chests heaving.

I'm starting to drift off to sleep when she places her fingertips on my shoulder.

"We should probably clean up, sleepyhead," she whispers. Her face is still flushed, sweat glistening on her chest, her curls wild and messy around her head. She's perfect.

"Yes, ma'am," I murmur with a tender kiss to

her temple.

"You have a good weekend?" Wolfie asks, his voice as even as ever.

He doesn't suspect a thing.

"Yeah." I choke out my response as we head toward the conference table to join the guys for our weekly team meeting.

We're in the back office, overseeing product development as always. Except not quite as always. Because most days, I haven't just fucked Wolfie's younger sister over the weekend.

"What'd you do?" He folds his hands on the table, watching me.

"Not much." Another lie. They come so easily to me now.

Guilt swarms inside me. As much as I try to pretend I have it all together, I'm nervous as hell. My heart pounds inside my chest.

What's the end game here? What happens when Wolfie finds out? Or when I hurt Maren without meaning to? Because that's bound to happen when you don't know what the fuck you're doing. And I don't. I don't have a fucking clue.

I sit down at the conference table next to Wolfie and cross one ankle over my knee.

Act normal.

Mental images of the other night with Maren sneak their way into my brain. Her creamy skin, her rosy cheeks. Her fingers cupping her breasts while I feasted between her legs like she was my last meal.

Breathe, Hayes.

It doesn't matter how good the sex was. And trust me, what happened between Maren and me? It was fucking incredible. But that doesn't change one very important fact.

It was wrong, plain and simple.

It was one thing when we were just fooling around at the lake house. But it was another thing entirely to do what we did the other night. It was premeditated. The hotel room she'd booked. The condom I'd brought just in case. There's no going back from that. It's done. I can't take it back.

I release a slow breath as panic threatens to overwhelm me.

A feeling bubbles up inside me—a feeling so

big and wild, I immediately know what it is. But I won't name it. I can't. Things between Maren and me are just physical, and they'll run their course. They have to. And when that happens, I'll walk away. Just like I always do.

I can't change what happened. But I can control what happens going forward.

Aside from Rosie, I don't have any family. The only place I feel at home is with the guys. Wolfie. Connor. Caleb. Ever. They're my family. Which is why I can never fuck over Wolfie.

He and I go back years. The others I met in college, but Wolfie and I have been best friends since the third fucking grade. And Maren? Maren was the gap-toothed kindergartener with a too-big backpack. God, that thing almost toppled her over. I always promised Wolfie I would help look out for her, help take care of her.

Not take advantage of a schoolgirl crush and fuck her into next Wednesday the first chance I got.

"I'll be right back," I say as casually as I can.

Wolfie doesn't look up and grunts in response.

I head to the single-stall bathroom and pull out my phone. If this isn't a sign that what I'm doing is wrong, I don't know what is.

Maren's contact is one of the first that come up, and I start typing out a text message explaining that we can't do this anymore. That this weekend was a mistake. That I'm sorry.

But then I remember the look on her face at the lake house when she thought that I was the one who invited Holly. The look on her face that night when she thought I was rejecting her. This is the kind of news that will crush her, especially after what we just did. What kind of man would I be if I didn't tell her this face-to-face?

I delete the text and stuff my phone back in my pocket.

My heart hurts at just the thought of what I know I have to do. But also, for the first time, I know that what I'm doing is right. That ending things with Maren is the only way we can all go back to normal and move forward with clear consciences.

So, why do I feel so low?

Fourteen

MAREN

When Scarlett insisted we celebrate the fundraiser's success with drinks, there was only one restaurant suitable for such an occasion. The Signature Room.

The restaurant sits on the ninety-fifth floor of the Hancock Building, overlooking downtown Chicago, the glittering lights of the skyline a stark contrast to the black expanse of Lake Michigan at night. The service is top-rated, and the food and cocktails are out of this world, according to all reviews. In Scarlett's words, it's fancy as hell.

A blur of texts ensued, swapping photos of outfit options and landing on logistics. Before long, the plan was finalized. Tonight, Scarlett, Penelope, and I would arrive at eight o'clock in our finest semiformal looks. We'd split the cost of a rideshare service so we could all drink our fill—no designated driver necessary.

When we step off the elevator, our heels click pleasantly against the hardwood floor. Scarlett wears a loose-fitting black jumpsuit that cinches at the waist, with red pumps and lipstick to match. Penelope is flaunting her beautiful figure in a coral slip dress that falls to the knee, sporting an adorable pair of nude kitten heels. Meanwhile, I'm wearing my favorite out-on-the-town number—a strapless gray dress with strappy black heels.

The hostess looks up from her clipboard and smiles a warm welcome before directing us to the cocktail bar in the loft above.

Walking up the winding staircase, I take in the view. The restaurant is even more elegant than the photos online. We find a small table next to the wall of windows, sharing excited giggles. Perusing the cocktail menu, I'm pleasantly surprised by how reasonable the prices are. Scarlett orders a dirty martini with extra olives, Penelope proudly flashes her ID and asks for a vodka soda, and I opt for a glass of white wine. As we sip our drinks, the conversation comes easily.

"It's honestly such a waste too." Penelope sighs. "We were having such good conversations. But I haven't heard from him in over a week. I can take a hint."

She smiles halfheartedly, and my heart aches for her. Her experiences with dating apps are thankfully less colorful than Scarlett's, but still not great.

"I hate that shit," Scarlett grumbles over the rim of her martini glass. "Just be up front, you know? As women, *we* should be the ones ghosting *them*. Men don't take rejection well. I'll admit, I've ghosted a few crazies over the years. But normally, if I'm just not feeling it, I tell him straight up. I don't understand why men can't return the courtesy."

"Exactly." Penelope splays her hands wide over the table as she leans forward to whisper, "I *know* we had a connection. So the least he could have done was respect my feelings and tell me he didn't want a romantic relationship with me. It sucks, yeah, but at least there's transparency."

"I swear you're both indestructible," I say, grateful for an opening to chime in. "I've never had any luck with dating apps. One weirdo, and I deleted all my accounts."

"I don't know about indestructible." Scarlett laughs, stirring the olives in her drink.

Penelope takes a long swig of her vodka soda before she says, "Yeah, speaking for myself, I'm not indestructible, just lonely."

"Girl, you've got us. Single women are the pioneers of the future," Scarlett says, raising her glass.

Penelope giggles, and I watch their glasses touch with a soft clink, uncertain if I should participate or not.

Am I single right now? Or are Hayes and I a thing? The question sparks a familiar tingle in my core.

Before I know it, both of them are staring at me. One of Scarlett's eyebrows is angled sharply in skepticism, while Penelope looks on with innocent interest.

"Unless some bitch here isn't single anymore . . ."

"Maren, are you seeing someone?"

My mouth goes dry, so I sip my wine and collect my thoughts. Before I can respond—*what can I even say?*—Scarlett gasps.

"Oh my God. *Please* tell me it's not Hayes."

I freeze, and it feels like my blood is rushing backward. "Um, no. Not Hayes." I scoff, staring into my wineglass, hating that I have to lie.

When Scarlett sighs in relief, I'm a little disgusted with myself.

"Oh, thank God. I was gonna say, Wolfie would *kill* him. He'd kill both of you."

Penelope laughs nervously while I frantically search for the waiter. My glass is nearly empty, and I'm tempted to just ask him to leave me the whole bottle.

"Sorry, girl." Scarlett chuckles, waving one hand as if to shoo the thought away. "I don't even know why I thought that. There is no universe in which Hayes would commit, not even to a catch like you. He's just shortsighted like that, I guess. A lovable jackass, am I right?"

"Totally." I choke out the word, my throat tight with emotion. Leave it to Scarlett to shine the glaring light of reality onto my stupid, twisted fantasies.

Penelope must be very perceptive, because she jumps in, saving me and the moment. "So if it's not Hayes, then who are you seeing, Maren?"

"Oh," I say, trying to keep my quavering voice steady. "Just a guy I met through a work friend. We grabbed coffee a few times, but I'm pretty sure he's not interested in me because he wouldn't put his phone down."

Wow, who knew I was such a con artist? The lie does the trick, however, because Scarlett slams her drink down with another groan.

"I hate *that* shit too. Like, give me the goddamn time of day, dude. Dump his ass, Mare. You deserve someone who's going to prioritize you and only you."

I smile, raising my glass, my fist curled tightly under the table. "To guys who care."

"Wherever they may be!" Scarlett says with a snort.

Our glasses raised in solidarity, we all agree without words to down the rest of our drinks. To my surprise, when the waiter comes back not a minute later and asks if we'd like to order more, it's Penelope who responds.

"Another for us, please!" she says, squeezing Scarlett's hand. When her eyes meet mine, they're soft and understanding. "And how about the rest of the bottle for my beautiful friend here?"

Turns out Connor's little sister is a mind reader.

The car ride home is full of cheerful conversation. At some point, we're all snickering loudly about some sexual innuendo Scarlett has made about "the back seat," and somewhere in my wine-brain, I make a mental note to tip our uncomplaining driver generously.

Penelope is dropped off at her apartment in Lakeview first, blowing us kisses from the front stoop of her apartment building. I'm next, just north in uptown. When I open the car door to step out into the cool night air, Scarlett hops out with me, asking the driver to wait for "a hot second."

She wraps her arms around me tightly. "You know you can tell me anything, right? I will never, *ever* judge you. You're my best friend."

My eyes are filling with tears before I can fully process anything past the bear hug. "I know, Pinky," I whisper, using the nickname I called her back in college. "I love you."

"I love you too. Now go inside," she says, spinning me around and smacking my butt.

I dutifully scurry inside my apartment, stopping to wave from the open door before the car takes her even farther up north. My phone dings once I'm inside the building, notifying me that my rideshare is complete. I tip the driver thirty percent, the wine making me as generous as I am dizzy.

After stumbling up the stairs, I spend what feels

like five minutes trying to unlock the door with the wrong key. When I find the right one, I push the door open triumphantly, dancing my way inside.

All those years of college parties and underage drinking taught me one crucial rule above all else: *Drink your weight in water before going to bed.*

Stripping off my heels and my dress in the front hall, I plod across the floor in my underwear, grateful again that I make just barely enough money to live alone. I fill up my biggest water bottle at the filter and chug half the contents before filling it back up the rest of the way. Drunk I may be, but hungover? No, thank you.

It's not until I'm brushing my teeth and staring at my own reflection that I remember Scarlett's jarring words from earlier this evening. They vibrate through me with every pulse of my electric toothbrush.

There is no universe in which Hayes would commit, not even to a catch like you.

How many times did I stand here, envisioning the domestic fantasy of Hayes and me brushing our teeth together before bed? How often have I imagined sharing the same space, the same *life* with my brother's best friend?

Something in my stomach churns violently. I

hurriedly spit out my toothpaste, awaiting the inevitable rush of sickness. But nothing comes. It's just my own stress, wreaking havoc on my body. All over one guy.

A small voice in my head cries, "He's not just any guy! Hayes is the only guy who's made you feel this way."

I silence the voice of the romantic little girl inside me that should have died when I first got my heart broken back in college. Staring at myself in the mirror, my mascara running, toothpaste smeared across my cheek, I look completely lost. I'm not sure when I started crying . . . but there's no stopping it now.

Somehow, I manage to wash my face, strip off my bra, and slip into an oversized cotton T-shirt. Snuggling under the covers, I imagine a version of myself on the other side of all this drama. It's the only thing that lulls me to sleep.

Fifteen

HAYES

Nothing could have prepared me for this moment.

When I texted Maren to meet me for coffee on Sunday afternoon, I knew what I had to do. I knew why I had to see her.

But sitting here across from her, watching her pull the sleeves of her sweater over her palms, watching her run her fingers through her long chestnut-brown hair—that's a whole other story. I don't know if I can do what I came here to do. She's too sweet, too innocent. What I'm about to do will break her.

But that's exactly why I have to do it. Because the longer this goes on, the harder it will be to end it, and ending it is the right thing for both of us.

So, why is it so damn hard for me to get the words out?

I drum my fingers on the table and watch the ripples in my black coffee. Maren smiles weakly on the other side of the wooden slats, her hands wrapped tightly around her latte mug. The smell of warm cinnamon rolls wafts by, fresh out of the oven, and a slow, soulful song plays softly over the speakers. I chose this place for a reason. It's warm, comforting. Anything to soften the blow.

"I've never been here before," Maren says, half to herself, her gaze trailing along the mosaic behind me. "It's nice."

"Best-kept secret in the city." I try to sound casual and cheery, but it comes off forced and canned.

Maren smiles in response, but this one doesn't meet her eyes.

She knows. I can't keep the thought from bouncing around in my head as panic spreads from the pit of my stomach all the way to my toes. If I don't do it soon, I'm afraid I'll lose my nerve.

"So, uh, Maren, I wanted to talk to you about something."

She flinches at the sound of her name. I'm not the only one who noticed I didn't call her "dove."

She nods for me to continue, her mouth flattened into a tight line.

"I wanted to talk to you about what happened between us. It was a mistake. One we can't repeat." I say the words quickly, my voice flat and emotionless.

It's like all the air has been sucked out of the room. Like I'm the one who sucked it all out.

Maren stares at her latte, her hands still wrapped tightly around the mug. So tight, her fingertips are starting to turn white. "Okay," she says without looking up.

"I'm sorry if—"

She stands abruptly, her chair legs scraping against the floor. "I have to go." Before I can stop her, she turns and bolts out the door and makes a left, heading straight for the train.

I sigh and scrub my hands roughly over my face. Customers around me are murmuring, but I can't bring myself to care. I feel like I've just been socked in the stomach with a baseball bat, but also like I was the one who swung the bat.

Way to go, Hayes. You've hurt Maren.

Back at my place, I find Rosie sitting at the kitchen table with a book in her hands. She smiles and peers over her reading glasses when she sees me, the corners of her eyes crinkling softly.

"You look like shit," she says. We've never been the kind of family to mince words with each other.

I sit down across the table from her and say nothing. She stares at me, her thin eyebrows raised on her wrinkled forehead.

"I'm really feeling like pizza. Can I take you out for pizza?" I ask.

Sitting down has made me antsy. I immediately want to stand back up, to get out of this apartment. I need to move, to do something to keep me from thinking about what just happened. I doubt I could eat, but Rosie is always easy company.

"I'd love to get a slice from Pauly's." The smile on Rosie's face is casual enough, but I can tell in her eyes that she knows something is up. Lucky for me, she doesn't ask any further questions.

We drive in almost complete silence, nothing but the radio playing between us. I can sense Rosie scanning my face, but I ignore it and keep my eyes on the road. I'm not ready to talk to her about what happened. It's too fresh. Too raw. Hell, I barely know what I'd even say about it.

When we get to Pauly's, I've just placed our order and gotten Rosie seated at a table when my phone starts buzzing in my pocket.

I pull it out to find Wolfie's name on the screen. "Hello?"

Rosie furrows her brow. I mouth Wolfie's name to her, and she nods and waves her hand in understanding. "Tell him I said hi," she whispers.

I nod and try to focus on what the hell Wolfie wants.

"Maren's not answering her phone. I need you to go check on her."

Hello to you too, Wolfie. "Why can't you?" I ask.

Rosie waves a hand in front of my face. "Is it Maren again?"

Since when is Rosie so damn perceptive?

"Because I'm on a date," Wolfie says gruffly.

Wolfie? A date? What the fuck is happening right now?

"Of course we'll go check on Maren. Don't you worry, Wolfie," Rosie says loudly, leaning in to speak into my phone.

Fuck. I can't even be mad at Rosie. She has no idea that I just broke Maren's heart. But that doesn't change the situation.

"Thanks, Rosie. And thank you, Hayes. You're a good friend," Wolfie says.

"Wolfie says thank you," I repeat to my grandma, and she nods and reaches over to pat my knee. But inside, I feel hollow and numb.

Wolfie shouldn't be thanking me; he should be beating the ever-loving shit out of me. But instead, I get to keep running around playing knight in shining armor. And this time, I'm taking my grandma with me. *Yay.* Nothing awkward about that.

We take our pizza to go and head to Maren's. Rosie waits in the car while I walk up to the door. My heart pounds with every step closer I take. I knock, but no one answers. I knock again. Still nothing. When I get back in the car, Rosie gives me a confused look.

"No answer?" she asks.

I grip the steering wheel and watch my fingers go white. "I know where she is."

I take us east. Maren's always had the same place she goes when things get hard. The same place she's retreated to when some asshole hurt her, when she needs somewhere to be alone. I never would have thought that I'd be the one to send her there.

We pass a sign that reads **MONTROSE BEACH**, and I park and tell Rosie to wait in the car.

She places her soft, warm hand over mine and gives me a small smile. "Go get your girl."

I smile back at her weakly. If only she knew what those words really meant.

A cool breeze greets me as I make my way to the beach. Waves crash gently in the distance, and it doesn't take long until I spot Maren huddled into a tiny little ball a few yards away on the sand.

When I get closer, she hears me coming and shoots a curious look over one shoulder. Her eyes are swollen from crying, and she gives me a blank look as I approach.

Ouch. I deserve that.

"I have nothing to say to you," she says, curling her arms tighter around her knees and facing the waves again.

"Wolfie's worried. He asked me to check on you."

She scoffs. "That's why you're here? Fuck off, Hayes. We have nothing to talk about. Call my brother and tell him I'm fine."

She rises and begins brushing sand off her pants, ready to walk away, when we both hear the sound of another set of footsteps approaching from behind me.

"Is my grandson the reason you're upset?" It's Rosie, wrapped in her cream-colored knit cardigan, the breeze lifting her thin gray hair.

Maren looks at me in surprise, then to Rosie. "I'm sorry, Rosie. I didn't know you were here."

Rosie clucks her tongue and slides her arm around Maren's shoulders. "Get in the car, little one. We can sort this out without everyone catching a cold."

"She's right," I say. "I think it's starting to rain." The breeze has picked up, and I've definitely felt a few drops fall.

Maren glances between us, and Rosie gives her a reassuring look.

"I've got some cookie dough ready to be baked in the fridge, and I'll brew us all a hot pot of tea the second we walk in that door."

Maren nods and lets Rosie guide her to the car.

The whole drive home, I can't help but feel uneasy. What am I supposed to say to Maren? And how did Rosie see right through me?

I can't keep my gaze from drifting to the rearview mirror to steal a glance at Maren in the back seat, but she just stares straight out the window, looking anywhere but directly at me, it seems.

When we get back to my place, Rosie makes good on her promise. Within ten minutes, the three of us are sitting in my kitchen, the smell of cookies wafting through the air.

Rosie pours us each a mug of tea, quickly followed by a healthy pour of whiskey. "Can't hurt," she says with a wink.

Maren smiles and thanks her, but I can't help but notice that her smile doesn't reach her eyes.

I down my mug in one gulp. The heat and the whiskey burn down my throat. It's exactly what I need. Inside me is all kinds of turmoil. Half of me wants to fix things between Maren and me, and the other half vows to remain strong.

Rosie pulls the cookies from the oven. As she arranges them on a plate, she instructs me to get Maren something dry to wear. I go to my closet and grab a pair of sweatpants and a T-shirt, and Maren takes them into the bathroom to change.

Rosie pours me another mugful of tea, and I add in more whiskey this time. She arches a thin, wispy brow at me, but says nothing. My stomach hasn't stopped churning all night, and I'm hoping a little more booze will help drown out some of the noise.

Maren returns, and my heart drops out of my chest. It's not fair. She can't look this beautiful in my T-shirt and sweats. Especially not after I just told her we can't be together anymore.

"It's getting late," Rosie says, glancing between us, "or at least, it's late for me. I'll leave you young folks alone. Good night, you two. Don't eat all the cookies." She kisses my forehead and pats Maren on the shoulder before slipping into her room and closing the door.

Silence falls between us. The whiskey's made me a little tipsy, and I can tell Maren is too. Her cheeks are flushed, and when she looks at me, her lids are heavy over her hazel eyes.

"Please, dove, can we talk? I have a lot I need to say to you." My voice is even, but on the inside, I'm wavering. It hurts my heart to see her like this.

"Okay," she says in a small voice, her arms crossed over her chest. "I'm listening."

I touch her shoulder to guide her to the couch.

It's an innocent gesture, but the second we touch, I feel a jolt of something. It's bittersweet, and I inhale and try to gather myself as Maren takes a seat.

I sit down beside her and slowly release the breath. She watches me, quiet.

"I've never felt about you the way I should have," I say slowly, meeting her eyes. "My feelings were . . . far from brotherly. There was always an attraction there, one that I fought hard to turn off. But I never should have acted on it. I know that now. I was only trying to protect you."

"From what?" She blinks.

"Me."

Maren shakes her head ever so slightly. "I'm a big girl, Hayes. I don't need protecting."

She's right, I realize. She's an adult. We both are. We can make our own decisions.

Suddenly, the tension that's been building between us all night snaps. Everything else fades away, and it's like we're back at the lake house. All that matters is the two of us. And there's too much room between us.

I lean closer and she falls into my arms, her hands grasping at my chest as our mouths collide, all heat and desperation. This is what I've wanted from the moment I spotted her on that beach. This is what I've wanted from the moment I let her go.

I guide her into my lap and lose myself in the moment. My hands in her hair, her hands on my chest, our bodies intertwining. Everything is exactly as it should be, as it always should have been.

And then it hits me.

Rosie.

"Not here, dove."

I scoop Maren up in my arms, and she squeals and buries her face in my neck. That's the kind of sound I want to hear more often. I've got a few ideas about that. I carry her into my room, making sure to close the door gently behind us, and lay her down on the bed.

Nothing else matters now. Not Wolfie. Not my grandma. Not even what I thought was right or wrong just this morning. Nothing that feels this good, this perfect, can be wrong, can it?

I take off my shirt, and she does the same. Our eyes are locked as we watch each other undress, me standing at the foot of the bed, Maren splayed out before me. She tosses my sweatpants in the corner, and a small smile forms on her lips. My body responds instantly as my cock springs free from my briefs, pressing up against my abdomen.

"You're so beautiful," I murmur.

She props herself up on her elbows to watch me move closer. My cock twitches in anticipation, and this time, she definitely notices. Her smile widens, and her eyes grow hungry as I lie down next to her on the bed.

We kiss again, deeper and more intensely than before. I reach between her legs and brush lightly over her center. She shudders, smiling into my mouth, and responds by giving my balls a gentle squeeze.

"Careful, dove," I growl.

She kisses me harder and takes my cock in her hand. Pleasure spreads throughout my body from her touch. When I push her away, she looks up at me with confusion in her eyes.

"You first," I say, placing my hand between her legs.

Maren moans, and I draw circles over her sensitive spot, watching the pleasure rock through her body. When I know she's ready, I slide inside her, and we make the kind of love I've only ever heard about in songs. The kind of love so good, so in sync, it's hard to imagine ever doing it with anyone else.

After we finish, she cleans up in the bathroom and stands in the doorway, looking hotter than hell in one of my T-shirts.

Holding a strand of hair between her fingers, she says, "So, should I—"

"Stay," I say before she can finish asking. "Please. I want you to stay."

She climbs into my bed next to me and curls into my side. The moment we're settled, I can feel myself drifting off to sleep, content knowing that she'll be there in the morning when I wake up.

"Oh, Maren! I didn't know you were still here."

Nothing makes me feel more like I'm sixteen all over again than surprising my grandmother with a girl in the morning. But this isn't just any girl. This is Maren. And the fact that she's still here right now, sneaking out of my bedroom? Well, that's pretty much our smoking gun.

Rosie gives us both an amused smile, and Maren blushes so hard, her whole chest turns red.

"Good morning, Rosie," she says meekly, taking a mug of coffee and sitting down at the table.

Rosie chuckles and pats her on the arm. "No need to be sheepish around me, sweetheart. I was young once too, you know."

I shoot her a look, and she shoots one right back at me. *I live here too*, Rosie's eyes are telling me, *and don't think I don't know what's going on here.*

"So, uh, Rosie, any big plans for the day?" Maren asks, clearly desperate for a change in subject.

"Probably another day of soaps and your favorite books, right, Grandma?" I ask.

Rosie shrugs. "Am I that predictable?"

"You should come to Riverside," Maren says, half to herself.

"Oh no, I wouldn't want to impose," Rosie says.

"No, you wouldn't be an imposition at all. Guests are always welcome at the community center. It's bingo day today, if you're willing to try your luck." Maren smiles widely at her, and I can't help but smile watching her.

"Well, I *do* love bingo," Rosie says.

"So you'll come?" Maren's practically about to

fall out of her chair.

"All right, I'll come."

Maren squeals and pulls Rosie in for a hug. It's nice, seeing them like this.

"I'll drop you both off," I say.

"Well, I need my car," Maren reminds me.

"Okay, so I'll drop you both off at your place so you can drive, and then I'll come pick Rosie up when bingo's done."

"Okay." Maren gives Rosie a smile. "Bingo will be done at eleven. And don't worry, Rosie, we'll take great care of you at Riverside. We've got coffee, pastries, fruit. Whatever you might want, there's a good chance we can make it happen."

Rosie smiles and looks between us. "Oh, don't worry, dear. I'm not worried at all. In fact, I have a very good feeling about all of this."

Sixteen

MAREN

"I've always said that Hayes should settle down with a nice girl like you."

Rosie peers at me through her cat-eye glasses, popping another mint from the jar on my desk into her mouth. She's graciously agreed to let me stop by my office and send out a few emails before dropping her off at bingo. But now, comfortably seated in the chair across from my desk, she seems to be entirely uninterested in giving me any quiet time for concentration.

"Rosie," I say, regretting the long-sleeved dress I put on after Hayes dropped us off at my apartment. It's suddenly *very* warm in here. "I don't know if—"

"He's a real sweetheart, my grandson. And a gentleman, when he makes the effort. I've always told him that if he'd just treat a young woman like he treats his grandmother, he'd have been married by now. Although I don't mind the attention," she says with a giggle, one hand resting on her heart.

A smile slips through my defenses. There's something so disarming about Rosie . . . you can't help but tell her all your secrets.

The truth is, I like where Hayes and I are right now, in this sort of *friends with benefits, will-they-won't-they* scenario. I can't know for sure if it'll last longer than one of his typical summer flings.

I try very hard not to think past our next hookup. I'd much rather think about the mind-blowing sex we've been having, the complete abandon in which I give my body over to his hungry mouth and hands.

Memories of his thick length, pounding me into oblivion, awaken a familiar tension deep in my belly, grounding me back in the present where the innocent old lady across from me is clueless to my dirty thoughts. A little reluctantly, I close my laptop, giving Rosie my full attention.

"The truth is, I really like Hayes. A lot."

Rosie chuckles. "I can tell."

I swear this room's temperature has spiked ten

degrees since we got here just fifteen minutes ago.

"I think Hayes likes me too. Well . . ." I pause, thinking. "He's at least attracted to me."

"I doubt there's a difference in Hayes's head," Rosie says knowingly, and I feel my heart clench.

Doesn't she know that she could be setting me up for the disappointment of a lifetime?

"True," I say, scratching my temple. Rosie leans closer, and unconsciously, so do I. "It's just that he's never really been the commitment type. There's always been something holding him back."

She's nodding before the words are fully out of my mouth. "There has been. But once he's with the right girl, none of that will matter anymore. Believe me, I know."

With a slow sigh, I lean back. As wise as she is, I have no idea if Rosie's right about this one.

I clear my throat. "Well, enough talk about all that. Ready to win some high-stake rounds of bingo?"

Rosie angles a single wiry eyebrow, but says nothing more. Instead, she collects her purse and gestures for me to lead the way.

My guest seems to like Riverside even more

than I do. Bingo isn't until ten, and Rosie isn't one to wait around, so she insists I give her a tour of the facility. She's fascinated with every nook and cranny as I walk her down each resident hallway, through the medical ward, past the courtyard, and back into the main corridor, finally stopping in the media center.

But when we walk through the double doors of the game room, I spot a handful of aides rearranging the seating, and remember that a summer camp choir is joining us this morning.

Making sure that Rosie is comfortable by the room's small kitchenette, brewing herself some tea, I help seat the residents who wander in one by one. Some are confused, others grumpy, but the majority are eager for another exciting event to take place. The group of thirty or so kids is a total hit with our residents, visiting from a local children's summer camp for the second time this week.

Lucky for us, our fundraiser allotted Riverside a lot more than just money. With the press coverage and corporate involvement, the attention on our little operation has rejuvenated both our financial status and our programming. Even the alderman's office is involved now. There's a consistent stream of messages in my in-box, small business owners and HR departments asking how their company can contribute.

If the local children's choir isn't visiting, then vendors are dropping by to donate fresh fruits, veggies, jams, and cheeses in a simulated farmer's market, reminding our memory-care residents what it's like to shop for groceries. One of the neighborhood's art collectives even visited last week, providing all the paint, brushes, smocks, and canvases to make a glorious mess of abstract art pieces now hanging along the walls of the main corridor. I'm most excited about the after-school "Reading Buddy" program we'll be offering come late August, where school-age kids will read to our residents, and vice versa.

Before long, a few dozen residents are crammed into the room, wheelchairs and sofas rearranged to serve as audience seating. At nine thirty, the kids file in, wearing matching green polos and khaki shorts.

Scanning the room, I find Rosie standing where I left her, but she's not alone anymore. Don, world-class charmer that he is, leans over his own cup of tea and murmurs some joke that has Rosie positively rocking with laughter.

"Uh-oh, that can't be good." I chuckle, approaching them with my arms crossed over my chest and a playful sternness to my voice. "I see you've met Don, Rosie. Don't believe anything he says, especially if it's concerning the meatloaf."

"We hadn't gotten that far," Don exclaims in mock-earnest, turning to Rosie to ask, "Have you ever seen the 1973 movie *Soylent Green*?"

I don't understand the reference, but Rosie laughs uproariously. My heart fills with joy. It's rare that you get to watch a friendship bloom between two people right before your eyes. I don't think I've ever seen Don so charismatic, or Rosie so carefree.

"Where have you been hiding this treasure, Maren?" she asks, dabbing at her eyes with a napkin. "He's an absolute riot."

We're the only ones still talking when the choir director steps forward, pointedly clearing her throat into the microphone before introducing the children.

Giggling like preteens who've just been reprimanded, we sneak into the back row and squeeze onto a sofa. The music is lovely, even when the kids forget the words to a shortened version of "Let It Be" by The Beatles. When they start their third and final song, I have to nudge Don gently with my elbow to keep him from interrupting the singing with another quip to Rosie. He shoots me a look of mild disdain. I smile and give him a wink before nodding my head toward Rosie.

"One more song, okay? Then you can get back to flirting."

"Who *me*?" he asks, but the smirk on his lips is impossible to miss.

The students' version of "Ave Maria" is a bit pitchy, but none of the residents seem to mind in the slightest. I hear a sniffle to my right and turn to find Rosie tearing up at the final notes. When the applause begins, she shoots off the sofa, hooting and hollering for an encore. While a handful of our more reserved residents appear rattled by the outburst, the excitement dominoes down the rows until nearly the whole room is chanting for more. The poor choir director looks flustered, fumbling through her folder of music.

"I'm sorry," she blurts into the mic. "That's all the music we've prepared."

"Do you know 'Twinkle, Twinkle, Little Star'?" Don calls out.

The kids nod emphatically, and one shouts, "Duh!"

"Yes!" Rosie cries, clasping her hands over her heart. "Please sing for us, little stars."

I'm pretty dumbfounded myself, but I have to admit that these two seem like peas in a pod. When the choir director leads a shaky-at-best rendition of the nursery rhyme classic, Don and Rosie share a triumphant smile. For the first time in my life, I'm honored to be a third wheel.

Neither Rosie nor Don are as interested in bingo as they are in each other, so I let them wander into the courtyard together, chatting up a storm. When my phone rings at a quarter till eleven, my heart skips a beat at the name lighting up my screen.

Hayes.

"Hey," I say, running a hand through my hair.

"Hey, dove." His low voice sounds yummy over the phone, like warm melted honey. "I'm about to leave to pick up Rosie, but she isn't answering her cell. Is everything okay?"

I chuckle, peeking out the window to see Don belly-laughing at one of Rosie's snarky comments. "Everything is totally fine. She's just distracted."

"Pretty heated game of bingo, huh?"

"Actually, she's really hit it off with one of the residents. They're taking a walk in the courtyard right now, and they'll be grabbing lunch together in the cafeteria in a bit."

"Oh God." Hayes sighs. "Don't let Rosie bore her friend with tales of her quilting adventures."

"From the looks of it, Don is hanging on to every word." There's a long pause on the other end. "Hayes, you still there?"

"Yeah, yeah. Is that Dawn, as in *A-W-N*—or Don, as in *O-N*."

"*D-O-N*. He happens to be my favorite resident. It's really sweet—they've become fast friends."

Another pause.

"Huh." Hayes's voice sounds strangled.

What could be bothering him? It isn't like Hayes to be so curt with me.

"What is it?" I ask.

"Rosie hasn't gone on a date in like sixty years, Mare."

I laugh, relieved that he's just weirded out by the situation and not upset at me for letting his grandmother off the leash. "Then maybe it's time she get back in the saddle."

"Oh God, no mention of saddles," he says with a groan. "My grandmother won't be riding anyone or anything."

I chuckle and murmur an apology. "Bad analogy. My bad."

Hayes grumbles something softly. I can't tell if he's actually agitated about her meeting Don, or just thrown off by this news.

"Well, there's a first time for everything," I say with a smile.

"I guess," he mumbles. After another awkward silence, he adds, "I'll swing by around one, then. Does that work for you and *D-O-N* Don?"

Oh my God, he's really irked by this! I have to bite the inside of my cheek to keep from poking any more fun. "Of course. See you soon."

"Yep," Hayes grumbles.

I pocket my phone, beaming from ear to ear. Outside in the courtyard, Don and Rosie are seated closely together on a bench in deep conversation, serious expressions on their faces. Rosie places one hand on Don's, a gesture of compassion.

This is going to be awesome.

When Hayes arrives, I meet him at the front door and escort him to the cafeteria, where Don and Rosie are huddled together at a small table, thick as thieves. Hayes freezes at the sight, so I give him a soft pat on the shoulder before pulling over two chairs to join them.

"Hello, Don. I'm Rosie's grandson. It's nice to meet you," Hayes says stiffly, offering his hand to Don like a robot might.

Don accepts the handshake, his expression stoic save for the signature sparkle in his stormy blue eyes. "No formalities necessary, Hayes. Your grandmother has spoken of you and only you for the past three hours, so I feel like I already know you."

Rosie giggles, swatting Don on the arm. "Oh, stop it. As if you didn't show me a whole photo album's worth of your students' graduation pictures."

"Only because you asked," he says with a wink.

From the way she melts, I can tell that Rosie is absolutely smitten.

"I'm impressed," I say. "Don is a man of mystery. For the longest time, I didn't even know if he spoke."

"You're new here, kid," he mumbles with a smile, a faint blush spreading across his wrinkled cheeks.

I can't help but clasp one of his warm hands between mine and give it a gentle squeeze. "That's how he tells me he loves me," I say, clarifying for the group.

"I see. Is he taken?" Rosie asks, humor twinkling in her eyes.

"Not at all, Rosie." I sigh with feigned disappointment. "Don turned me down years ago."

While the three of us laugh, Hayes shifts uncomfortably in his seat. I guess I should try to bring him into the conversation. But before I have the chance to come up with a strategy, he finally opens his mouth.

"What do you do, Don?"

"Oh, a little bit of this and that. Crossword puzzles and afternoon naps, mostly."

"Ha," Hayes says with a fake laugh. "I meant before Riverside. What did you do for a living?"

"I was a college professor at U of M, teaching the classics. Roman and Greek history, literature, et cetera. Lucky for me, your grandmother is quite the mythology buff herself."

Hayes says nothing in response, staring him down like he's deciding whether it's morally reprehensible to beat up an old man.

I reach under the table to rub his knee comfortingly. *Relax.*

"What do you do?" Don asks, genuinely interested.

Uh-oh.

"I own a sex-toy shop here on the north side." Hayes's voice is loud, proud, and brimming with cockiness. He probably thinks mentioning anything openly sexual will scare Don away. Clearly, he doesn't know the man.

"Fantastic," Don says in a low voice, clapping his hands softly together. "I have about a dozen erotic posters for you to look at—renderings of ancient Roman frescoes. I'm not allowed to put them up here. Would you want to put some of them up in your shop?"

Hayes is stunned into silence, his mouth twitching. Meanwhile, Rosie and I share a pleasantly surprised look.

"That would be perfect for the shop," I say, jumping in. "They could make a collage on the back wall."

The conversation continues easily from there, Hayes pitching in now and then in an attempt to recover his pride. I know that all he wants is to be sure Don's intentions are pure, but there's still time for that.

At the end of our visit, Rosie and Don say their good-byes with the promise to have another date on Saturday.

"We should have a double date," Rosie exclaims with a confident expression that boasts of her problem-solving superpower. She and Hayes really are blood relatives, aren't they?

"That sounds fun," I say with a smile.

And it really does. On a double date, I can get in all the cute couple-watching I want, and Hayes can monitor the progression of their relationship. Not to mention that I've been itching to spend more time with Hayes, in *and* out of bed.

Don waves good-bye from the front doors as Hayes helps his grandmother into the front seat of the car. I'm about to turn around and head back indoors when his hand reaches for mine, spinning me back around. His fingers play lightly with the buttons on my dress, sending shivers across my skin.

"Hey," he growls softly, with the sexy little smirk he reserves just for me.

"Hey." I giggle back, a little breathless.

"Can I take you out tonight? No double date. Just the two of us." His tongue peeks out to wet his bottom lip.

I run one finger between his pecs, down his cotton T-shirt, appreciating the firm feel of his chiseled torso. "I'd like that," I murmur, the twitch in my core impossible to ignore.

"Good," he whispers, leaning in to press his full lips against mine in a hot, eager kiss that ends way too soon. After he releases me, he heads back to the car and starts the engine.

I watch as he and Rosie drive away. I'm still cemented to the spot where he left me when I hear Don approaching me from behind.

"Seems like a handful, that one," he says with a grunt, patting my shoulder.

I'm not sure if he means Rosie or Hayes, but either way, my answer is the same. "You have no idea."

Seventeen

HAYES

I haven't been this nervous for a date in—well, ever. Wining and dining have always come easy to me. That's my sweet spot. But doing this with Maren? When the stakes are so much higher than they ever were before? It's a whole new ball game.

I want tonight to be different. *Special.* I want Maren to feel worshipped like she never has before, like no man has ever made her feel. That's why tonight, I've got more than one trick up my sleeve.

"So, where are we going again?" Maren's brow furrows slightly, making the faintest little crease between her eyebrows.

She's sitting in the passenger seat, wearing the kind of low-cut emerald-green dress that makes me want to pull over and pull her onto my lap. But for now, I push those thoughts aside and stay focused on navigating us through rush-hour traffic.

"Out," I say, lacing my fingers through hers over the center console.

She smiles and clucks her tongue. "Are you going to be elusive and mysterious all night?"

"Well, that depends. Is it working for you?"

She blushes, and I can feel the heat from her palm. I know what blushing does to her. Her chest will turn pink, and her breathing grows rapid. I'd love to investigate what's happening between her legs, but tonight is about anything but instant gratification. It's about pacing ourselves and luxuriating. Tonight, we're going to take our time.

Something has shifted between us recently. Maybe it's how close she's growing with Rosie, or maybe it's because I got to see her in her element at Riverside. Now that I've seen her in her environment, I can't imagine that place existing without her.

Maren breathed life into the old tiled hallways. She brought hope and positivity and joy. She's special in so many different ways I never knew about.

Around old people? I'm awkward. People who are sick and in pain? Hell, I'm useless. I never know the right thing to say. But Maren shines like she was born to do this, to help them relive their best memories, to help them transition into a new chapter with grace. She's comforting and funny and so natural, I have no idea how she does it. I'm damn proud of her.

We arrive at the restaurant, and I pull up to the valet. Maren's eyes grow wide, and she stares at me in horror, ignoring the man waiting to open her door and help her out of the car.

"Hayes, this is too much. This place is so fancy! This is like, where my grandparents went for their fiftieth wedding anniversary."

I nod and give her a reassuring smile. "And this is where you and I are having dinner tonight."

"Are you sure?"

"They have this crème brûlée that I'm almost positive will be your new favorite dessert."

She pauses, chewing at the inside of her cheek. "Okay, fine. But I really wish you would have told me we were going somewhere so nice. I would have worn better shoes."

"Dove, you could be wearing a trash bag and still be the most beautiful girl in the entire city. These assholes are lucky to have you inside their establishment."

She blushes again, and this time I'm fortunate enough to watch the flush spread over her. God, she's fucking gorgeous.

Down, boy. Pacing is going to be harder than I thought.

We're escorted inside the lavish building by the doorman, and once inside, are met with a bustling dining room full of white tablecloths and a view of the city I haven't seen in a while. Twinkling lights of the buildings in the distance, and beyond, the dark water of the lake.

Maren lets out a soft gasp, and I place my hand on the small of her back as a hostess leads us to our table next to the floor-to-ceiling windows, just as I requested. We order a bottle of wine for the table, and the server nods before setting a basket of sliced bread between us. When he leaves, Maren looks at me, her eyes still wide and slightly glazed over, a small, pleased smile forming on her lips.

"This is . . . exquisite," she says softly, looking wistfully from the basket of bread to the view beside her.

"Well, don't speak too soon. We still have to see if they get the steaks right." I grin.

"No, Hayes," she says, taking my hand over the table. "I—I want to thank you. I haven't had a night like this in a very, very long time. So, thank you. Really."

I give her fingers a gentle squeeze. "You're welcome. Really."

We lean in and kiss over the table, and I can just catch the sweet vanilla scent of her perfume. I didn't realize that being here would mean so much to Maren, and it makes this night all the more important.

"Well, in that case, please tell me that you're hungry."

She smiles and arches a challenging brow. "Starving."

We have what's probably the best steak dinner I've had in years, complete with all the classic sides. I order us the crème brûlée for dessert, as promised, and just as I predicted, it's immediately Maren's new favorite dessert. She groans around the spoon, and her eyes sink closed.

Everything is going exactly like I hoped it would. Luckily for me, our night is only just getting started.

I drive us back to my place for a nightcap.

A soft smile settles on Maren's lips on the drive home, while my hand rests on her knee, my fingers wandering idly over her thigh. When we park, it takes everything in me not to drag her into my lap and kiss the daylights out of her.

Patience, Hayes. I have to remember what I have planned for us.

Once inside, Maren looks at me expectantly. She glances around the kitchen, whispering, "Is Rosie . . ."

"She's asleep," I whisper back. "I'll meet you in my bedroom. Can I get you anything? Water? Wine? Whiskey?"

She shakes her head and pulls me in by my lapels. We kiss, and she rubs her hand along the growing bulge at the front of my pants. "Don't be too long."

Don't have to tell me twice.

She slinks away to my bedroom, untying the straps to her dress before slipping behind the closed door. Such a little tease.

I pour myself a glass of water, and before heading into the bedroom, I go to the linen closet by the bathroom. There, behind neatly folded piles of towels and bedsheets, I find what I'm looking for—

a sleek black box, about the length of my forearm. I pull it down from the shelf and take it into the bedroom with me.

When I close the bedroom door behind me, I find Maren sprawled out on the bed in nothing but a pair of lacy pale-green panties. My cock's instantly rock hard and in a fight with my pants to get to her.

I let out a low whistle between my teeth. "Fuck, dove. You're going to give a man a heart attack."

A coy smile curls on her lips. "I wanted to surprise you. And thank you properly."

I set the water glass on the desk in the corner and hold the black box behind my back. "I have a surprise for you too, dove."

"Oh?" She props herself up on her elbows, her perky breasts teasing me.

I sit on the edge of the bed at her feet. She watches me closely as I lay the box on the bed in front of her.

"What is it?" she asks.

"Open it."

She takes the box in her hands and lifts the lid, her brows raising as she appraises its contents. "Oh," she says as she pulls a long curved cylinder out of the box and holds it in her hands.

The deep crimson silicone is striking against her pale skin, and a pulse of excitement courses through me at the sight of the toy in her hand.

Understanding washes over her face. "*Oh.*"

"It's one of our newest models," I say. "When I saw it, I immediately thought of you."

She nods, still staring at the toy in her hands.

My mouth is suddenly dry, and I have to swallow to get my vocal cords working again. "Would you like me to show you how it works?"

Maren lifts her chin, and when her eyes meet mine, they're heavy with lust. She nods again and hands it to me.

I instruct her to lie back, and she does, parting her knees, offering herself to me. My mouth waters at the sight of her pussy, shaven bare. I let out a low hiss.

"Looks like those panties are missing something, dove. Something very important," I murmur, unbuckling my belt.

She nods again and opens her legs wider. Crotchless panties. This girl will be the death of me.

"Have you been wearing those all night?" I tug my shirt off and toss it to the floor. "Answer me."

"Yes." She sighs and runs her hands along her sides.

Watching her writhing on top of my sheets, watching her turn herself on—it's almost enough to do me in. I pull Maren close, so her hips are at the edge of the bed, and turn the toy on.

The low hum of its vibration brings a gleeful smile to her lips, and I start by pressing it into her inner thigh. She groans softly, and I move the toy over her body, everywhere except where I know she wants it. Her legs, her belly, her chest. I even circle her nipples until they turn into hard little pebbles, and she's begging me to touch her most sensitive spot.

I move the toy to her clit with one hand and grasp her hip with the other. She's so wet, so ready, so deliciously turned on, and I can't wait any longer. I hold the toy against her as I move so I'm spooning her from behind. She's so wet now that I easily work my swollen cock into her heat. Maren gasps at the invasion and clutches my ass.

We rock into a rhythm until she's wild and sweating, her body squirming under my touch. Her body clenches around me, and she pulls the toy from my hand and takes control of her own pleasure, riding me and the toy in equal measure. She's so sexy like this, all confidence and taking charge, and I can feel my balls tightening.

"Dove, I'm close."

She grinds harder into me, and another wave crashes through her. Pleasure rips a cry from her throat, and I feel her contract around me. *Fuck, that feels good.* She tosses the toy onto the bed next to her as I finish, gripping her hips tightly as I come.

We collapse onto the bed, beads of sweat lining my forehead and chest. Maren slips my shirt around her shoulders and goes to the bathroom to clean up, and when she returns, she cuddles warmly into my side.

"That was incredible," she whispers. "Thank you. For everything."

"No, thank you, dove. Thank you."

"No, really, Hayes, how'd you fucking do it?" Connor squints at me with disbelief.

It's the next day, and instead of spending it in bed with Maren, I'm at work, surrounded by a bunch of assholes with the maturity of twelve-year-olds. But what did I expect? We started a sex-toy company together. Talking about our sex lives is literally part of each other's business.

Except when you're fucking your business partner's little sister, that is.

"Don't worry about it, all right? I got it done. That's all you need to know." I hardly look up from my laptop while I reply, but Connor and Caleb aren't buying it. They scoff and look at each other in disbelief, just in time for Wolfie to join us in the back office.

Great. Just what I fucking needed.

"What are you two idiots giggling about?" Wolfie asks, his voice slightly less gruff than usual.

"Hayes did some product testing over the weekend," Connor says.

"So?"

"*So,*" Caleb says, "he's sworn off women. So, how is he testing the product?"

Wolfie drops the box he's been carrying onto a shelf with a loud thud. "Well, some of our toys are optimized for solo use."

"Unless Hayes is suddenly very into anal," Connor says, his eyebrows shifting, and I cut him off.

"Fuck you, man."

Wolfie chuckles. "Whatever floats his boat."

I heave out a sigh. "The product is solid. Since when do we grill each other for details?"

Caleb raises his eyebrows and crosses his arms. "Dude, the only woman in your life is your grandmother, so unless you want me to puke up my protein shake, please explain yourself."

Connor and Wolfie laugh, but I just shake my head and keep crunching numbers.

"Fuck all you guys," I mumble. But at this point, between that option and the truth, I'm honestly not sure which one is worse.

Eighteen

MAREN

In preparation for our evening out on the town, Rosie and I spend the afternoon shopping at my favorite consignment store. Summer in Chicago is unforgiving, so the dress we select for her is a lightweight navy-blue number with a collared neckline, short sleeves, and a bold pattern of yellow flowers.

Meanwhile, I'm on the hunt for a little special something. When I see it, I know without a doubt that it's exactly what I need to keep Hayes nice and occupied. Summery and fun, the ruby-red romper showcases my long legs in a way that'll definitely have him reeling. Add a pair of strappy black sandals and a flirty ponytail . . . and he'll be a goner. I can hardly wait.

"You're gonna give my poor grandson a heart

condition." Rosie chuckles to herself as we check out.

The smile on my lips refuses to fade as we finish up at the store.

Back at the apartment, Rosie bashfully asks if I'll help her get ready. The invitation warms my heart, so I dutifully follow her down the hall to her bedroom.

The zipper slides easily up the middle of her slightly hunched back, a clasp securing it at the base of her neck. The ankle-length pleated skirt brushes against the pantyhose she insists on wearing, the entire ensemble pulled together by a pair of matte-blue Mary Janes from her closet.

I peek over her shoulder, looking in the full-length mirror to confirm what I already know. She looks lovely.

"My goodness." Rosie giggles, pulling at the fabric restlessly. "You sure this isn't too modern for an old fuddy-duddy like me?"

I grin at her use of the term *fuddy-duddy*. Can't say I've heard that one in a long while.

"Yes," I say to assure her, gently squeezing her shoulders. "You look perfect. It's got that Jackie Kennedy class with a little modern chic to it."

"Thank you." She chuckles, her berry-painted lips stretching into a shy smile as she turns to meet my eyes. "Thank you, dear. Tonight is . . . well, I'll just say that I haven't gotten ready for a date in decades."

I wrap her in a hug, careful not to smudge her meticulously applied makeup. "You bet."

There's a knock behind us, and Hayes's voice travels through the door, filled with annoyance and impatience. "Hey, are we doing this or what?"

I roll my eyes. "It's not even time yet, Hayes. We'll be out in five minutes."

Rosie shoots me a knowing wink. She sees through his attitude as clearly as I do. He's been a pill ever since meeting Don at Riverside.

I would give Hayes a piece of my mind about it, but I know he's just uncomfortable. For the past several years, he's been Rosie's number-one caretaker, confidant, and companion. It has to be hard to imagine someone else getting close to his grandmother, especially a stranger.

Meanwhile, I'm just happy for the both of them—Don especially. He's been considerably less of a grump since meeting Rosie. Over the past few days, he's gone out of his way to "casually" run into me in the halls of Riverside, resulting in impassioned conversations about Rosie's favorite flowers, Rosie's favorite movies, Rosie's favorite foods. It's cute.

After running the details by me, Don decided on a full evening of activities, which includes a trip to the local historic movie theater, a pit stop at the neighboring ice cream parlor, and a walk down to the lakefront to watch the sunset.

I'd be lying if I said I wasn't a little impressed. Who knew he was such a romantic?

Hayes and I are accompanying them, on the basis of it being a double date. But we all know the double-date spin is a total facade for fundamental logistics. Hayes doesn't want Rosie driving after dark, and Don hasn't owned a car in at least a decade. Furthermore, the logistics are just an excuse for Hayes to spy on Don the con man, who appears to be armed with nothing more than a few jokes and a listening ear.

Regardless of how Hayes spends his energies this afternoon, I'm choosing to see it as a double date. A double date in which I get to spend more time with the hottest guy I know.

When Rosie and I are finished, we step out of her bedroom to find Hayes waiting on the couch, his knee bouncing nervously as he scrolls through his phone. When his eyes meet mine, they immediately wander down the length of my body, taking in my high ponytail, exposed shoulders and collarbones, cinched waist, and finally—my long, tanned legs. His knee stills, his phone forgotten in his hand while he ogles my cute and sexy summertime look. His lips part and then shift into a cute half smile.

Hayes doesn't look too shabby himself, wearing a pair of comfy army-green chinos and a short-sleeved white button-up. We share a look that says, *You look good. Like, really good.* I'd relish the moment for a smidge longer, but we're on a timeline. Plus, I'm pretty sure Rosie wouldn't appreciate me eye-fucking her grandson right in front of her.

Piling into the Lexus with Rosie comfortably in the back seat, we drive to Riverside to pick up Don. When we pull into the circular driveway, he's waiting just inside the front doors. His hair smoothed back, he wears a light blue sweater with brown slacks and a golden-yellow bow tie. A bouquet of daisies are clutched in his hands—Rosie's favorite, naturally. My heart swells from the cuteness of it all.

Don is the picture of a dapper gentleman, only dropping the act to shoo away a hovering CNA. I step out of the car to sign him out for the evening, then help him into one of the back seats, shooting him a congratulatory wink as Rosie coos over the flowers. I'm amazed we make it to the movie theater at all with the way Hayes is white-knuckling the steering wheel.

By some brilliant turn of fate, or some excellent foresight on Don's part, *Soylent Green* is the old film of the week. Our adorable charges are eager to find the perfect seats, so I take Hayes by the hand and pull him toward the concessions stand.

"All right, Mr. Chaperone, time to let the kids off the leash," I say, teasingly bumping him with my hip.

His arm wraps around my waist, his hand slipping into the pocket of my romper to rest his fingers on the sensitive bump of my hip bone. A shiver floods through me at the contact, my body thrumming with the memory of those skillful fingers operating that sex toy. Ever since that experience, I've been feeling reckless . . . and a little wild.

"No kids here," he says, flashing me a smile that's more of a grimace. "From what I can tell, that's a full-on old dude staring at my grandmother's butt."

I laugh at the implication, because Don would sooner die than get caught staring at a woman's backside, proper gentleman that he is. "You're right, they *are* adults. All the more reason to trust them to take care of themselves, hmm?" I ask, rubbing his back comfortingly.

"I didn't say that I don't trust Rosie," Hayes grumbles, scanning the overhead menu. "I just don't think that she always knows what's best for her."

All right, Operation Reassurance is going to take a little more effort than I thought.

Hayes buys four small bags of popcorn, declining my suggestion with a pointed look to let each couple share a large bag. We sneak into the theater just as the lights dim and the movie crackles to life on the projection screen.

Rosie and Don are already engrossed in the experience when we find them. It's a special showing, so there are no previews to deal with. Settling into the two open seats behind the couple, I'm prepared to kick the back of Don's seat every time he nods off. Miraculously, he never does, too busy whispering in Rosie's ear, who smothers her uncontrollable giggling with mouthfuls of popcorn. They are *too* cute.

Hayes's knee bounces incessantly for the first half of the movie. When I've finally had enough, I reach out and place a hand on his knee, gently rubbing the tense muscles I find there. At my touch, he slowly begins to relax, giving in to the massage.

Hayes leans back in his seat with a soft sigh, subtly checking on our companions.

When the movie ends, our little group piles out of the theater and walks a few blocks to the ice cream parlor. Don and Rosie walk a few steps ahead of us, wrapped up in their own conversation about the plot of the movie.

They're clearly quite taken with each other, and from my experience working with people their age, that's not very common. Usually, distrust and prior baggage can form communication barriers between the elderly. That's not true in Don and Rosie's case, though. Their excitement and fondness for each other fills my insides with syrupy warmth, threatening to ooze out of my very pores. Finding love is always an amazing thing. Getting a second lease on life at their age is rare and extra special.

Meanwhile, Hayes is a little less stiff than before. As we walk, his hand wanders from my waist to the round swell of my ass, tracing lazy, feather-light lines just underneath the hem of my romper to play with the edge of my panties. It's enough to drive me absolutely crazy with desire.

The summer sun is already lowering over the peaks and valleys of the neighborhood rooftops and steeples as we arrive at the ice cream parlor. Don insists on paying, purchasing two scoops of rocky road for himself, one scoop of mint chocolate chip for Rosie, and one scoop of chocolate espresso for me. Hayes opts out, probably in quiet resentment of Don's kindness.

When the older couple wanders toward the beach to catch the sunset, promising to return within the hour, Hayes whispers in my ear. "Why eat an ice cream cone when I can just watch you?"

We settle into a small booth in the back of the parlor, our legs winding together underneath the table. With my back to the counter and any other patrons, I make a whole show of it.

Hayes watches me with darkened eyes as I lick and suck away at the swirl of soft serve with a vigor I can only attribute to being majorly turned on. I let a little cream drip down my bottom lip, meeting his eyes as I run my tongue lazily over one sticky finger. That's all he can take. He wraps a hand around the back of my neck and pulls my messy mouth to his in a hungry kiss.

Just then, someone's kid drops his ice cream cone with a wail—the perfect distraction.

I grab Hayes's hand, pulling him from the table and down the hall to the thankfully empty (and clean) restroom, where I practically shove him inside and close the door behind us. He's on me almost before I can latch the door, his hands grasping my ass and his lips devouring mine as I fumble for the lock. Once it clicks into place, I push him against the wall, dropping to my knees to nuzzle against the strained fabric of his shorts.

He groans, loudly this time, digging his fingers into my updo and ruining my hard work in the best possible way. In moments, he's unbuttoned and unzipped, his thick length free from his pants. I kiss a hot, wet path along his sensitive flesh, and Hayes makes a strangled sound.

"Fuck, dove . . . *Fuuuck*," he says breathlessly, his low voice crackling like hot coals.

The desperate sound of him, the hot, hard feel of him in my hands, is enough to drive me crazy. But I know I'll get my reward later, so I focus my efforts on making Hayes lose his mind. And he does . . . quickly.

"I'm gonna come." His fingers loosen their grasp, giving me an out if I need it.

I don't back away and swallow him even deeper. When he finally catches his breath, I'm gazing up at him.

"Holy hell," he says with a chuckle. Helping

me to my feet, Hayes wraps me in his arms, warmth radiating from him like a bonfire. He mumbles against my neck, "I messed up your hair."

"That's okay." I smile, nestling against him. I have so much affection for this man, I could burst.

"I needed that." He sighs, leaning back to meet my gaze. "Thank you."

"Anytime," I say with a smile, pressing a light kiss to his smiling lips.

"Can I return the favor tonight?"

I nod once, my heart rate picking up at the idea of Hayes on his knees before me, treating me to white-hot pleasure. "Of course."

His smile widens, and his eyes dance mischievously on mine.

Once we've collected ourselves and I've repaired my hair, we sneak out of the bathroom and back out through the busy ice cream shop. The cashier is too busy mopping up that little kid's mess to be concerned with us.

We make our way outside, and it's nearly dark out when the couple of the year returns, only separating their clasped hands to wave once they spot us at the edge of the beach. Hayes and I wave back, and Rosie cocks her head in response to his lazy smile.

"You really have a way with my grandson," she says as they approach. "He's so relaxed after a little alone time with you."

She reaches out to pat Hayes on the shoulder, who barely manages to keep his game face together. Meanwhile, I'm as red as a stop sign. She doesn't know the half of it.

The drive back to Riverside is oddly pleasant. Hayes invites Don to sit in the front seat with him, and I gladly join Rosie in the back. The men share an awkward but sweet conversation about the best things to do in Chicago, while Rosie and I share an awkward but sweet look of appreciation. *He's trying.*

When we arrive, Rosie insists on walking Don back inside. I crawl up to the front seat, a tangle of knees and elbows that sends Hayes diving for cover.

"Why didn't you just get out and get back in?" He chuckles, brushing some dirt off his shoulder from my shoe.

I laugh, shrugging. "Do you care?"

"No," he says, a sexy little smile spreading across his face.

He reaches out, his fingers tracing my jawline before he presses his thumb softly against my chin. It's a simple, chaste gesture, but it sends a warm wave of pleasure through me.

When Hayes looks out the window again, his smile drops like a bag of bricks. I follow his gaze to see Don and Rosie sharing a good-night kiss, and my heart explodes.

"Oh my God," I whisper, bouncing in my seat. "That's sooo cute."

"It's not cute, Mare. It's weird. And ballsy, but not in a good way. I don't know this guy. For all I know, he's just trying to steal Rosie's social security checks."

I angle an eyebrow at him. "Does Rosie have a sizable pension or something?"

He sighs, running a hand through his hair in frustration before mumbling, "No."

"Hmm." I lean over, patting him softly on the thigh. "You may not know Don, but I do. So you don't have to trust him. You can just trust me. Okay?"

Hayes struggles with this for a moment. Truthfully, my patience is wearing thin.

"Tell me what's really worrying you."

He sighs softly. "I'm worried about what every man is worried about when his grandmother falls in love with a ninety-year-old man."

My eyes narrow on his. "Him dying?"

Hayes scoffs. "Him breaking her heart."

"Relax, babe," I mutter, wishing we could just skip ahead to the part where everyone's chummy.

"*Babe*?" he asks, turning to me with an amused look that overpowers the discomfort that was threatening to set up base for good.

Oops . . . I guess that's one way to make him feel better.

"Is that okay?" I ask cautiously. Maybe I took it too far.

"No, it's great." He gives me a big grin. "Just unexpected."

"Says the guy who regularly calls me *dove*," I shoot back with a sly smile, walking my fingers up his chest.

With a mischievous grin, he catches my hand, bringing my fingertips to his mouth to bite them softly between his teeth. I gasp, snatching them back and clutching that chiseled jaw I've spent decades daydreaming about. His eyes glitter in the moonlight, growing darker as he leans in. When he speaks, his voice is wrapped in velvet.

"I thought you liked that."

"Who says I don't?"

Our lips are just a breath apart when the back door pops open and Rosie eases herself inside with a satisfied sigh. We pull apart reluctantly, Hayes clearing his throat as I crack the window open for a little more air flow.

"Oh, don't stop on my account. We didn't stop on yours," Rosie says matter-of-factly, humor in her innocent expression.

Hayes shudders, shaking his head mournfully as he starts the car. I have to bite my lip to keep from laughing. Or high-fiving Rosie. Or kissing Hayes.

Lucky for me, there's plenty of kissing once Rosie goes to bed.

Pressed up against the door of his bedroom, I let him have his way with me, kissing me deeply, urgently. I feel dizzy, drunk on his scent and taste. When his hands wander from my waist to my ass, hoisting me up against his tented pants, I let out a little squeak of surprise. Hayes smiles deliciously against my lips.

"No need to be quiet." He leans in to nip at my neck, and I gasp, my back arching and breasts pressing against his chest. "We're all alone on this side of the apartment. Besides, Rosie takes out her hearing aids every night."

"Isn't that dangerous?" I say softly, trying to focus despite the molten heat in my core, pressed against his rock-hard erection.

"That's what *I* said. What if the fire alarm goes off?" He sighs, his fingers slipping under the hem of my romper to play with my cotton panties, which are already damp. "Doesn't matter to her. She says she can't sleep with them in."

My eyes widen.

"Let's stop talking about Rosie." With that, he spins me around and deposits me on the bed with a gentle *whump.*

My heart rate accelerates as I watch him un-button his shirt and gaze down at me with hungry eyes. "I'll bet you've got this down to a science," I say, blinking up at him.

"Got what down?" he asks, pulling the tie of my romper slowly undone.

"Having sex . . . *here*."

He pauses, his eyes flickering up to mine. "I've never brought anyone else here."

"Really?" I ask, equal parts shocked and touched. That doesn't seem possible.

"Nope," he murmurs, lowering himself over me to pepper soft kisses along my collarbone.

"You've really never brought a hookup here before? A girlfriend?"

Hayes sighs, sitting back on his heels and running a hand through his mussed hair. "No one but you . . . and you're not a hookup, dove."

I pull myself up until I'm level with him, wrapping my arms around his neck to kiss him hard on the mouth. He groans against my lips, his hands settling tightly around my waist as he grinds against me. When we part, we're both breathless.

"You're killing me, sweetheart," he murmurs.

He reaches around me to pull my ponytail down, allowing my hair to spill over our shoulders. With his fingers tangled in my hair, his kiss is softer now, sweeter, as if I'm truly precious to him.

Tugging at my romper, he whispers against my lips, "Now, let's get you out of this damn thing."

My heart rate skitters. My savage is back.

We kiss and grind together in the center of the bed until I'm so ready and turned on, I can barely breathe.

"I know you have a toy stash somewhere," I murmur between kisses.

He meets my eyes with a heated look. "What makes you say that?"

"That toy you used on me . . ."

He smiles. "I only brought that home to test."

That might be true, but I'm undeterred, "Come on, you own an adult store. Just tell me. I'll find it." I grin at him, giving him a sassy look.

"Over there, second drawer down." He tips his chin toward his nightstand.

Pushing up on one elbow, I lean over the side of the bed to pull open the drawer. There are only two things inside—a bottle of lube, and a pair of fuzzy-lined handcuffs that seem more gag gift than anything. The store tag is still attached, which tells me these have never been put to use.

I grab the bottle that's about half-full and hold it up. "Lube? Hmm. Do you use this when you jerk off?"

He quirks a brow at me. "Yes."

My heart jumps. For some reason, the thought of Hayes with his fist around his cock, stroking himself in wet, jerky thrusts, is such a hot visual.

I flip open the cap and drizzle some of the unscented oil into my palm. When I wrap him in my fist, his wide chest stutters out an exhale.

"Fuck, Maren." He's so sexy like this, lying beside me, completely at my mercy. His voice is deep, barely more than a growl, when he says, "Tighter."

I tighten my grip and work him over until he's panting and groaning out deep, delicious sounds. His hands explore my body while I continue my sinful torture, slowly bringing him to the brink and back again.

When Hayes can't take any more of my sweet torture, he moves on top of me. Covering my body with his, he thrusts forward, filling me with a powerful stroke.

Clutching him tightly, I say a silent prayer that whatever luck I've found to win him over never runs out. I'm falling hard and fast, and can't imagine ever going back to being *just friends* with this incredible man.

Nineteen

HAYES

Things have been good lately. Too good, almost. It's making me suspicious. Antsy. Like at any moment, everything could fall apart, just like that.

Maybe that's why I'm so on edge these days. I keep finding myself flinching when someone opens a door too quickly, or when Wolfie calls my name from across the room. Even when I'm not with Maren, I can't quite seem to relax. It's really starting to mess with my head.

Don't get me wrong—Maren is incredible. My little dove is as potent a sexpot as ever. I'm the one who can't stop acting like a little kid who's afraid of going to bed without the lights on.

That's why I've decided to get away, just for the night. I packed up an overnight bag this morning and let Rosie know I was going to go check on the cabin. By sunset, it'll be me, a six-pack, and a bonfire sitting lakeside at the cabin. I'm hoping some alone time will help clear my head.

The workday goes by like any other. Ever and Caleb schmooze a few customers while Wolfie and I go over the new product line in the back. He's finally dropped the whole "how'd you test the new shit" act, thank God. I don't know how much longer I could insist that I wasn't fucking my grandma, without physically making myself sick.

You'd think I could have made up some kind of white lie or something to cover my tracks, but in my experience, any kind of deception, even something that seems small, will come back to bite you in the ass in the end. And I'm already in enough hot water with the Maren and Wolfie situation, I don't want to make things even more complicated by throwing a fake, imaginary hookup into the mix.

"Hey, man, you good?" Wolfie asks when he catches me eyeing the clock for the twelfth time today.

"What, me? Yeah, no, I'm good, all good here, bro," I stammer back. *Smooth.*

Wolfie gives me a disapproving look, but shrugs and doesn't press it any further.

Still, I have to say something. I can't just let it stay all weird like that.

"I mean, I'm just anxious to get out of here today, you know? Not that I don't love this job. Just really itching for some me time, you feel me?"

Wolfie shakes his head and chuckles dryly. "Me time. Sure, man, whatever floats your boat. Just remember that you've already taken your product samples for this quarter. We do track that shit, you know."

Fuck. Now Wolfie thinks I'm a grade-A perv. Whatever. Better than him knowing the truth, I guess.

"Ha-ha. Very funny."

"No, but seriously, dude, if you need a break, you should have said something. Why don't you skip out early?"

I stare at him in disbelief. Is this the Wolfie who started this company with me? The same Wolfie who created the schedule that gives me about three days off a year?

Then I glance at the clock. Four forty-five. All right, that makes more sense.

I slap a hand on his back. "Thanks, man. I appreciate your understanding."

He nods and continues typing away, only half registering my gratitude. But that's fine with me. Either way, I'm one step closer to my lake time and bonfire.

I spend the drive to the lake house going over all the possible scenarios of what might happen with Maren in my head. Historically, I'm not the kind of guy with the best track record.

Things just don't work out well for me. Hell, that's why I swore off women in the first place. And I can't help but worry that the same thing will happen with Maren, no matter how good and right things feel now. That epic breakup with Samantha throwing my shit out the window isn't a scenario I want to repeat again, and I couldn't live with myself if Maren ever hated me.

Because it's not like relationships ever start out obviously bad. Okay, maybe I've had a couple start out that way. But for the most part, I jump into things because of how perfect they seem on the surface. It's only once we start swimming deeper that I notice all the murkiness and sharp rocks waiting down below.

But Maren has to be different, right? She's not just some girl I met at a bar, or hell, even some girl I swiped right on from some app. She's *Maren*. Wolfie's sister. We've known each other forever.

That has to mean something. What I can't tell is whether what that means is something good or something very, very bad. Either way, I'm afraid of failure and need to get my head on straight.

By the time I pull up into the long gravel drive-way, I've worried myself into one huge ball of anxiety. *Fucking perfect.* The exact opposite of what I needed.

I lug my bag and the six-pack inside from the trunk, and when I flip on the lights in the foyer, all the memories of the last time I was here come flooding back to me. Maren and I were just start-ing out then. Hands brushing, eyes meeting. The sexual tension was so thick between us, you could have taken a bite out of it. Not that any of that has changed in the past couple of weeks.

The first beer goes down faster and easier than I expected, and the second is right behind it. I make a small fire in the pit by the lake as the sun starts lowering over the horizon. Its warmth and light are just enough to cut through the cool evening breeze.

Water laps at the shore, and I'm about to reach into my cooler for beer number three when I hear the sound of tires on gravel.

What the hell?

I didn't tell anyone to meet me here. And unless one of the guys also decided to go on a last-minute getaway, something tells me I'm about to have some unwelcome company.

"Hello?" I stand and call out.

The car parks behind mine and kills its lights. After a few moments, the driver's side door opens, and a pair of long, tanned legs pop out.

"Thought you might want some company."

It's Maren, dressed in a pair of cutoff jean shorts and a lacy tank top, looking sweeter than any fantasy I could have dreamed up.

"Jesus, dove," I wheeze out, half out of relief and half out of arousal. "Some warning would have been nice."

She sticks out her lower lip into a pout. "You're not happy to see me?"

I pull her in close, so the sweet scent of her skin mingles with the smoky warmth of the bonfire. I didn't realize I was lonely until the moment she arrived. She's right. It's nice to have some company. Especially when that company is my current favorite person.

With my hands on her waist, I lean in and kiss her. All that worry, all that fear turns into urgency between us. She wraps her arms around my neck and the wind lifts the ends of her hair. I'm lost in her, lost in this moment, and when we part, I couldn't tell you what I was so worried about before.

She rests her forehead against mine, and I release a sigh.

"Hey, you okay?" she asks, placing her palm gently against my cheek. The gesture is so soft, so tender, it takes me right back to that night at the lake house in my bed. When she took me by surprise by kissing me.

I nod and take a deep breath. "How did you know I was here?"

"Rosie told me. I went by your place after work to say hi and was surprised to find her all by her lonesome."

"Yeah. I needed some time . . . away."

"From me?" Maren asks, her voice small and timid.

"No, dove. From everything else. From the city. From your brother. The guys at work. It's all just starting to feel like too much."

She stares down at our feet. "Are you saying that this is too much? We're too much?"

I grasp her hands in mine and search her eyes. It breaks my heart to hear her even say those words.

"Dove, I want you so desperately, I can barely even contain it. It's the situation that's starting to make me feel crazy. You've watched me all these years, so you know—I'm not good at this. Things just don't work out for me. I mess up, I hurt people, and the last thing I ever want to do is hurt you. I don't know if I'd be able to live with myself."

"I told you, I'm a big girl. I can take care of myself."

"I know that. But I can't shake the bad feeling that this won't end well."

"You were never a bad boyfriend, Hayes," she says thoughtfully.

"What do you mean?"

Her eyes meet mine with a sincere look. "You just weren't with the right person."

I let her words sink in, and it takes me a minute to realize she's right. Maybe Maren is the person I'm meant to be with. No one else. That's the reason why I couldn't make a relationship last.

The heavy weight that's settled inside my chest eases slightly at that realization.

Maren cradles my face in her hand, her forehead pressing into mine. She doesn't respond, but I can feel the worry tracing lines across her skin. We hold each other like that for a while before putting the fire out and going inside.

I don't know where we'll go from here, but I do know one thing—for tonight, I'm glad we're together.

Twenty

MAREN

The nightclub is thrumming with life, filled from wall to wall with glitter-covered bodies, pulsating bass beats, and strobing lights. The scent of sweat hangs in the air, and I'm starting to question why I agreed to come out tonight.

Scarlett doesn't let go of my hand as she drags me through each room, making good on her promise not to leave me alone in here. It's not the first time I've been to a nightclub, but it's definitely not the kind of scene I frequent very often like she does.

Scarlett moves seamlessly through the throngs of dancing twenty-somethings, only stopping to touch the elbow of a woman wearing the same sequined dress and high-five her.

My look barely makes the cut for adequate club

wear—a black knee-length dress with lacy edges. Good thing Scarlett took one look at my sensible gray sneakers and ordered me back inside my apartment to find anything "with a little more sex built in." The black-and-white platform boots were an impulse purchase after a particularly difficult week at work, but now I'm happy to get the chance to wear them.

After we pass through what feels like the twentieth hazy, sweaty room, I spot Hayes and the other guys standing at a high-top table with drinks in hand. Scarlett hollers over the music, and all heads turn to see us approaching. She ditches me for only a moment to grab shots at the bar, having successfully delivered me to our friend group. Well, friend group, plus the one outlier I'm not sure how to categorize.

Hayes looks hot as hell in his dark-wash jeans and a simple black T-shirt, but when doesn't he look amazing? Flanked by Caleb, Connor, and my brother, Wolfie, Hayes can't do much more than give me a lustful look, appreciating my outfit with his eyes.

I'm debating walking right up to him and kissing him smack dab in front of everyone, secrets be damned, when I'm attacked from the side.

"Sorry! Didn't mean to scare you!" Penelope

giggles into my ear.

I'm a little shocked, but then I remember she's graduated from college and moved back to Chicago for good now. She's obviously making the most of it, two cups of beer pinched at the lip between her thumb and forefinger, and some bubbly mixed drink clenched in her other hand.

"I didn't know you were coming."

"Wolfie invited me."

Wolfie did what now?

"You look great," I said, and she really does.

Penelope's hair is done up in a cute topknot, and her adorable pink slip dress is hugging her body in all the right ways. She opens her mouth to return the compliment, but Scarlett bumps in between us.

"Take a shot," my friend urges, pushing some unknown alcohol toward my lips.

Making the quick decision that this will be my third and final shot this evening, I throw it back, cringing at the flavor. Of course it's tequila. *Yuck.*

"Atta girl!" she shouts. "Let's dance!"

Scarlett pulls me toward the dance floor, blowing a kiss to Penelope, who promises she'll catch up with us. She hands the beers off to Connor and

Caleb, who immediately start chugging, their competitive streak still going strong. I only manage to catch a brief glimpse of Penelope, nestling herself very close to my stoic-as-ever brother, before my view is blocked completely.

Scarlett spins me around, helping me find the rhythm with her hands resting lightly on my shoulders. Together, we swing our hips to the beat, losing ourselves to the music pumping over the speakers. Scarlett dances with complete abandon, verging on silliness, which I know she only does to make me feel more comfortable.

You don't have to be good at dancing to have fun at the club. And Lord knows I'm not much of a dancer . . . the last time I set foot on a dance floor was with Hayes, and it wasn't exactly the kind of music you'd bump and grind to.

With Hayes on my mind, I look back to see Caleb and Connor chatting up some pretty girls I don't recognize, and Wolfie and Penelope engrossed in a deep conversation. Hayes stands alone, resting his elbows on the table as he takes a slow swig of his drink, which I'd bet a hundred bucks is bourbon on the rocks. Even with the crowd, his eyes are trained on me—on my hips—as I dance.

The music shifts into something slower, headier, and the alcohol in my bloodstream makes me braver. Swaying from side to side, I run my hands over my thighs and waist teasingly. I like dancing for Hayes, and he certainly appreciates the show. He smirks, jutting his chin toward the far wall, where I spot a glowing neon sign for the restrooms.

Another covert quickie? I'm down.

I whirl around to find Scarlett dancing with a circle of strangers, neon body paint giving them an ethereal glow.

I lean in, shouting over the music, "I'll be right back."

"Where are you going?"

"The bathroom."

"Okay, I'll come with you."

Ugh, I didn't think about the club code. Always take a friend with you to the bathroom.

"That's okay," I say, knowing my protest will fall on deaf ears.

"Let's go." She waves good-bye to her new friends, because who knows if they'll cross paths again after tonight.

Reluctantly, I follow her lead across the dance floor and toward the restrooms. When I can hear myself think again, I grab her hand and gently pull her toward the wall. Her eyes are confused, but she waits for me to speak.

"I don't need to use the bathroom," I say, nervously crossing my arms over my chest. Is now the right time to tell her? I don't even know if Hayes and I are . . . well, *anything* yet.

"What's up? You don't wanna dance anymore?" She rubs my arm protectively, concern spreading across her features. Scarlett is seriously such a good friend. She doesn't deserve to be lied to, even if she doesn't approve of Hayes's dating habits.

"Not exactly," I say, taking a shaky breath. "I was going to meet Hayes."

"Hayes?" she asks, frowning. Suddenly, realization dawns on her face. "Oh shit, are you and Hayes a thing?"

I nod, my eyes prickling with emotion. What if she's hurt that I lied? What if I've just ruined the night? I swipe a single tear from my cheek, cursing tequila for always making me so damn emotional.

But Scarlett doesn't look hurt or angry at all. Instead, she smooths my hair and wraps me in her arms, squeezing me tight. "Tomorrow, when we do hangover brunch, you have a lot of explaining to do. For now, go have fun. I love you!"

She punctuates her words with a hard kiss on my cheek, and all the tension I've been carrying around falls away like a suit of armor I no longer need.

"Thank you. I love you too."

"Oops, I got lipstick on you." She laughs, licking her thumb and rubbing it away. "Go get him, girl. I'll find Penelope and actually get her on the dance floor with me this time." With that, Scarlett turns on her heel and heads back toward the table, where I'm sure she'll give Wolfie hell for hogging our favorite new friend.

I smooth my dress of any wrinkles and make my way past the tables of drunken clubgoers, all the way to the back where I find Hayes, leaning against the wall with a quizzical expression on his face. When I'm close, he reaches for me, tucking a loose strand of hair behind my ear, his hand lingering to cup my cheek.

"You okay? I thought you got lost."

"I'm great."

"Really?"

"Really."

"Good," he says, leaning down to kiss me firmly on the lips.

He tastes like bourbon. *One hundred imaginary bucks for me.*

The kiss turns fiery as I open my mouth, letting his tongue explore mine with the same curiosity as the first time we kissed. His hand ventures from the side of my face to my ear, sensually tracing the shape of it before sliding behind my neck, deepening the kiss. I press myself intimately against him, feeling him vibrate at my touch, his other arm wrapping tightly around my lower back.

My feet are nearly hovering off the ground when he breaks the kiss to ask, "You wanna get out of here?"

"For good?"

"Not if you want to come back."

"Okay," I whisper, capturing his perfect mouth in another searing kiss. I'd kiss this man 24/7 if I could.

Eventually, we untwine ourselves from each other long enough to find the exit into the alley, walking hand in hand toward the quieter, intersecting street lined with trees, coffee shops, and liquor stores. I lean against the brick wall, inviting Hayes to join me with a coy smile and a beckoning finger.

We're entangled in moments, a flurry of hungry mouths and greedy hands, pushing and pulling with the familiarity of long-time lovers. When my fingers press over the firm bulge in the front of his jeans, he catches my hand in his, a breathless laugh warming my neck where his kisses have stopped.

"What's wrong?" I ask, lifting one leg to wrap around his, pulling his hips closer.

He releases my hand, bracing against the cold brick, and rests his forehead against mine. "Not here, dove."

"Why not?" I ask, grinding against him with a smirk.

"C'mon, Mare . . ."

"No, tell me why," I demand, pulling my hips back. "I know you've gotten frisky with other girls in places like this, so it's not a principles thing. What is it?"

"Maybe I'm not trying to fill some void inside me anymore."

I scoff, more confused than upset. "What does that mean?"

He sighs, his voice low and pained. "I was only with those other girls because I knew I could never have *you*, Maren. But it never worked, because they weren't you. And now . . . well, things are changing for me. For us. I've never felt like this before."

The air between us is fragile, like it could catch fire or shatter like glass at any second.

I gently press my hands against his chest until we can look each other in the eye. With my heart in my throat, I ask the question that's been hanging in the air between us since that night at the lake house.

"Do you have feelings for me, Hayes?"

His eyes are stormy in the glow of the streetlight, their normal lightness darkened with inner turmoil. He doesn't look away, though, or clench his jaw, or fall back on any of his other avoidance techniques. He just looks at me. For a long time.

"Hayes?"

"I'm afraid if I say it, your brother is going to kill me."

"Scarlett knows, and she doesn't care. Wolfie won't either."

"You don't know that."

"Yes, I do," I say, grasping his shoulder tightly. His hands fall from the wall, his arms hanging limply at his sides, instead of around me where they're supposed to be. "Just say it."

Hayes drops his gaze to the cement, and I know all at once that I've pushed him too far. Now he's going to shut me out again, close the door for good to this beautiful thing we've discovered. But even if it crushes me, I need to hear the truth.

With a numb heart, I release him, taking one staggering step away. Before I can move another step, though, I'm tugged back, spun around, and captured between two strong arms.

Hayes buries his face in my neck and whispers, "I love you."

My heart lights up like a firecracker. I kiss him hard, gripping his hair between my fingers like it's my only tether to the ground, or else I'd rocket into the sky. When I look into his eyes this time, I don't see a storm. I only see the future.

"I love you too, Hayes Ellison."

Twenty-One

HAYES

My phone rings, cutting off the song I was blasting mid-chorus. Wolfie's name flashes across the screen. He probably wants to talk about the shop schedule or the new product line. I press ACCEPT and wedge the phone between my ear and my shoulder.

"Wolf, what's up, man?"

"Hey," he grunts, and then there's silence on the line. Leave it to Wolfie to call me and not tell me right away what he's calling about.

I release a slow breath and search for patience. "You still there?"

I put down the dishes I've been drying and listen for sounds of life. The line crackles, and I hear Wolfie clear his throat.

"So, you and Maren, huh?"

Fuck. Fuck, fuck. A heavy weight sinks to the pit of my stomach. This is not how I wanted this conversation to go.

"She talked to you?"

He grunts. I guess that means yes.

"Listen, Wolfie, I asked her not to. This isn't how I wanted you to find out. I wanted to be the one to tell you."

"What the fuck, Hayes? I thought I could trust you."

Another punch in the gut. This is going worse than I thought.

"I know. I'm sorry, man. I should have talked to you about this sooner."

"No shit. What the actual fuck? You need to start talking, and you need to start talking now. What the hell has been going on right under my nose?"

I sigh and run my hands roughly over my face. *Fine.* If Wolfie wants the truth, then it's the truth he'll get.

"All right, fine. Honestly? I'm a fucking kamikaze, man."

"You're a what?"

"A kamikaze. A suicide bomber. All those relationships I've jumped into and destroyed in the past? I sabotaged every single one of them."

He pauses. "Okay . . ."

"Because they weren't Maren. I've been in love with her for years. I was just too scared and too blind to do anything about it. I love your sister, man. And she loves me too. I hope you can accept that."

Silence again. I can practically hear my heart pounding through my chest.

Finally, Wolfie chuckles. "Then you should be with her. Treat her like a queen."

Relief floods my body. Every fear, every worry, every stress I've been holding on to for the past few weeks is gone in the blink of an eye. We have Wolfie's blessing. We can be together, for real, all the way now.

"I promise I will. Thanks, Wolfie."

He hangs up with a click, and I let the phone drop to the counter.

There's only one thing left on my mind. I have to go tell Maren.

Later that afternoon, I'm sitting in a coffee shop, one hand interlaced with Maren's, the other resting on her knee. We're across the table from Rosie and Don, who's starting to grow on me—even if it still makes my skin crawl to see his arm around my grandma's shoulders.

Rosie hasn't stopped smiling since we told her the news. Honestly, neither have we.

Having Wolfie's blessing means we can stop sneaking around and be a couple out in the open, something I don't think I realized my grandma was rooting so hard for. Hell, I think she was about ready to just go tell Wolfie herself if one of us didn't do it soon.

"Well, aren't the four of us quite a sight," Rosie says, a wide smile crinkling the corners of her eyes.

Don rubs her shoulder and gives her a peck on the cheek. If I weren't so damn happy about Wolfie's blessing, that's exactly the kind of thing that would have bugged me.

Maren runs her thumb over my fingers and gives me a reassuring look. She knows me so well. Too well, almost. That's what makes us such a great team.

"You know, Rosie, we wouldn't be here without you," Maren says with a grateful shake of her head. "Really. Thank you for believing in us, even when we didn't."

"That's my Rosie," Don says, beaming at my grandma. "She's a light."

Maren squeezes my fingers. I know what she's trying to tell me. *Don't even think about it. They're adorable. Let Rosie be happy.*

"I knew you kids would figure it out," Rosie says with a wave.

"Your meddling says otherwise," I say, half under my breath, and Maren swats my arm.

Rosie chuckles. "You two just needed a little encouragement, that's all. The connection between you was plain to see. To the trained eye, that is."

Maren and I exchange a glance. She smiles, and my heart squeezes. *God, I love this girl.*

"That right there, that look between you. It's precious. Hold on to that," Don says.

Rosie nods. "You'll need it. Along with kindness and respect. Your relationship will suffer without them."

Maren smiles. "Any other advice from your experience?"

Rosie screws her mouth up into a tight line for a moment while she thinks. Then it unwinds into a soft smile as she places her hand on Don's knee. "All that stuff about how you should never go to bed angry? Bullshit. Sometimes it's okay to sleep it off and try again in the morning."

My ears perk up. I was expecting a generic platitude. This is genuine, coming from someone who really wants to help us.

Maren and I turn our attention to Don, who's currently gazing at Rosie with the most admiration I've ever seen one person give to another.

"Always put the other person's needs first," he says, staring seriously into Rosie's eyes. "Even when it's hard. Even when it's uncomfortable. Even when you think your needs are really important. Love is sacrifice, and your actions should reflect that."

Wow. A real stunner of an answer from Don. I guess I need to give this guy more of a chance than I thought.

Rosie leans over and places a small kiss on his cheek, and Maren rests her head on my shoulder.

This isn't the kind of family unit I ever envisioned for myself, with just me, my girlfriend, my grandma, and my grandma's boyfriend. But right now, at this moment, the four of us feel like a family.

Of course, my family is more than this. It's also the guys I work with—Wolfie, Caleb, Connor, and Ever. They're my chosen family, the people I choose to be around. And Maren, well, she's the girl I chose a long time ago.

I can't believe how lucky I am to have her now. And there's no way I'm letting her go.

Epilogue

MAREN

"I'm gonna need a break after this," Caleb grumbles.

A very old, very heavy vanity is hoisted haphazardly over his shoulder as he follows Wolfie's lead up the stairs. I try to stay out of their way, only jumping in to make sure we don't do any damage to the antique, or to Riverside's wallpaper on the way up to Rosie's new apartment.

Rosie organized everything very neatly in preparation for the move, even offering to hire a crew. But, lucky for her, we have some beefy young men at our disposal already, the owners of Frisky Business eager to take the day off from the shop to do a little manual labor. Well, more likely it was the bribe of hot pizza and cold beer at the end of a long day that enticed them.

While Wolfie and Caleb unload the vanity and catch their breath, I pop said beers into the empty refrigerator and head back downstairs toward the truck. Scarlett stands in the bedroom, passing boxes down to Penelope as Connor slings garment bag after garment bag over his shoulder.

The apartment is fully furnished, so it was relatively easy to pack up Rosie's life in a matter of days, putting a hodge-podge of remaining items up for sale online. Don also insisted that she didn't need to bring any kitchenware, assuring us that he had enough for the both of them.

That's right—Rosie is about to move in with her boyfriend.

Hayes is taking the transition pretty well, having come a very long way since his first introduction to Don. It was only a couple of months ago that Rosie sat us both down for another whiskey-infused tea-time chat and told us her exciting news.

"Don and I would like to take the next step in our relationship, as you kids like to say. You've taken care of your grandma all this time, my dear. I'm very grateful to you." She then reached across the table to take both of our hands in hers, gently squeezing them. "Both of you."

"Don't you think this is a little fast?" Hayes

asked, genuine concern in his voice. "You've only known Don for, what? Not even a year?"

"Life is short." Rosie sighed, but her expression was cheerful. "I don't want to waste any more time worrying about the proper way to do this or that. Don and I love each other very much. We deserve to be happy."

Since then, Hayes has actively made an effort to spend more time with Don, signing him out of the nursing home to take him to baseball games and bring him to the shop. I'm proud of him, and honestly a little jealous of their budding friendship.

Rosie, I could handle. But battling Don for Hayes's attention? It brought me an unexpected wave of unease. But I knew this was going to be a good move . . . for all of us.

Rosie's deep laugh draws me back to the present, and I turn to find the three of them approaching, finally done signing the remaining paperwork. It seems to me that Rosie and Don have been holding hands since the moment they met.

The rest of the day passes quickly, a flurry of furniture rearrangements and pizza topping requests.

After we've called it quits for the night, I step away from the buzzing conversation and onto the apartment's balcony to call in our order. There, I find Hayes leaning against the railing, his eyes focused on the orange-and-purple tapestry of the setting sun.

"Hey," I say softly, leaning my head against his shoulder.

"Hey." He wraps an arm around me, pulling me against his warmth. There's nothing better than cozying up next to your favorite person after a long day like today.

"How are you doing?" I ask, looking up at him through my eyelashes. I can't quite read his expression. If I'm being honest, it's unlike any I've ever seen. Pensive, definitely. Hopeful too?

"I'm good," he murmurs, his striking eyes leaving the sunset to meet mine, somehow carrying that residual warmth with them.

"Yeah?"

"Yeah."

"Anything on your mind?" I ask, knowing that Hayes always needs a little push, that extra gesture of permission to let him know, *you can tell me anything.*

"Well . . ." He sighs, pressing his lips to my forehead. "I thought I'd have more time with her.

I don't know if I feel worse about keeping her cooped up in the apartment for so long, or for not spending enough time together, just the two of us."

"Hayes, you're the best grandson anyone could ask for. Rosie loves you so much." When he doesn't respond, I continue. "It's not like she'll be far away. We can visit her anytime."

"You're right. I know that." He chuckles, nuzzling his nose into my hair, and I nestle into him, savoring his masculine scent. "It's all happening pretty fast, huh?"

"Says the guy moving in with my sister."

We turn, surprised to find Wolfie leaning against the doorframe, his arms crossed over his chest. We both know him well enough to recognize when his scowl is the *I'm gonna beat you up* kind, or the *I'm just giving you a hard time* kind. Luckily, this time it's the latter.

"You order that pizza yet?" he asks, nodding toward the forgotten cell phone in my hand.

I suck in a sharp breath through my teeth, realizing I'd completely abandoned my mission. Being around Hayes does that to me. Always has, and always will.

"Sorry," I mumble, extracting myself from

Hayes's arms to finish what I started.

"Don't worry about it. I got it," Wolfie says, pulling out his own phone.

"You don't have to—"

But the phone is already pressed to his ear as he walks back inside to rejoin the others. It's less of a cold shoulder and more of a decision to let us live our lives in peace.

I look up to Hayes with a hopeless expression, and he simply grins down at me.

"Wanna take off after the pizza?" he asks, drawing my chilled hands between his and blowing his warm breath on them. "Go home?"

Home. My heart sings.

"And unpack more boxes? I don't know," I say with a sigh.

Yes, Hayes and I have already moved in together, not even a year since we exchanged *I love you*s. No, I'm not worried.

"I know a specific box we could unpack," he murmurs, one eyebrow rising suggestively.

I know exactly which box he's referring to. The indecent little collection of battery-charged pleasures we've accumulated over the past year. We haven't had a chance to play since we packed them away and shuffled them from one apartment to another.

A shiver runs up my spine, but not from the cold . . . oh, I'm *plenty* warm now. Our lips touch, so soft and tender that I'm tempted to take his hand and sneak him back to his car, where we can do more than just talk about sex.

"Oh yeah? That box?"

Hayes pulls me a little closer. "Mmm. I was thinking we'd stow it away in the nightstand. Easy access."

"We should probably leave one or two in the kitchen. And the living room. And the bathroom. And the car. Both cars. You know, just in case." I give him a flirty wink.

A rich, contented laugh resonates from deep inside him, wrapping me in love. "Whatever you want, dove. Whatever you want."

And I know he means it. Hayes would give me whatever I want—the whole world, if he could. It's a comforting feeling, and one I'm so incredibly grateful for.

Wolfie and Penelope's book is up next in *My Brother's Roommate*. Wolfie may be the most deliciously broken alpha hero I've ever written.

Next in This Series

There are a few things you should know about my brother's roommate.

Wolfie Cox is . . . *complicated.* Terminally sexy, and more importantly, he has an impressive stick lodged so far up his ass, he's about as emotionally available as a chinchilla. Actually, that might be an insult to the chinchilla community.

So, naturally, I want to ride him like a bicycle.

He thinks I hate him. Mostly because I've led him to believe this. It's easier than admitting the alternative.

And while Wolfie is about as soft and cuddly as a fork, I'm the opposite. A good girl. Reliable. Conscientious. Oh, and completely panicked about an upcoming work conference.

Wolfie's usually allergic to altruism, so when my brother asks him to help me out by escorting me to said conference where everyone else will have a plus-one . . . I say thanks, but no thanks. Surprisingly, Wolfie is unflinching about this. And that's the story about how I got stuck in a hotel with my brother's hot (*grouchy*) roommate.

Thank you for coming to my *TED* talk.

In all seriousness, this isn't a game to me, and hormones aside, I need to impress my boss this week so the promotion I've worked hard for doesn't get handed to his spineless nephew. But with Wolfie and me sharing a hotel bed, things get confusing quickly.

Deleted Bonus Scene

Enjoy this deleted scene from when Maren met Hayes
at the cabin in Chapter 19…

Inside the cabin, we find my bedroom. It's dark
except for the moon—which pours in through the
window, bathing its inky blue light over us. Standing beside my bed, I'm hopeful Maren can't tell
how nervous I am. How much indecision I'm filled
with. I came here to think, to make a choice and
force myself to see it through—no matter how
much it gutted me. Now though? With Maren and
I about to climb into bed, I'm less certain than before.

She lifts her face to mine and I press my mouth
to her neck, kiss her warm skin, breathe in her familiar scent. Though I told myself this wasn't what
tonight would be about, my dick begins to harden.

Her mouth finds mine and I'm weak, powerless to stop this. Kiss after hungry kiss, I let myself
drink in my fill. My hands explore, cupping her
perfect ass. She groans weakly into my mouth and
I deepen our kiss, my tongue sliding and tangling
with hers.

Jesus. Why is this so good? Why is she so hard
to walk away from?

With super-human strength, I pull myself away.

Maren blinks up at me. "Why'd you stop?" Her gaze is filled with lust and my brain short-circuits.

Why did I stop?

Because I don't want to ruin our friendship. Or my relationship with Wolfie.

But there's no one here to interrupt us, and at this moment, the only thing I'm sure of is my longing. Deep, drowning longing that screams at me from deep inside my being. It's primal—the need to claim her, mate with her ... have her in every way I can.

Maren doesn't wait for me to respond, she lifts on her toes and presses her mouth to mine once again. Her tongue coaxes, treating mine to soft, wet strokes while her hand presses into my cock.

It's like a fiesta of sensation.

We fall back onto the bed and begin scrambling with each other's clothes. It doesn't take long for me to strip her naked. I'm kissing one soft breast, my fingers pinching the nipple on her other as she wraps her fist around my cock. Her strokes are unhurried and I rasp out a breath.

"Feels good," I say on a groan, teeth lightly grazing the soft, plump flesh of her breast.

She makes a small pleasure-filled sound and arches her back, pushing more of her tit into my mouth.

God, I can't get enough of her. I arrange us on the bed so she's lying back against the pillows and I hover over her on my forearms. She's beautiful and I take a moment to tell her so. Her hands are everywhere—in my hair, on my waist, clutching my ass so that my dick presses into the wet flesh between her legs.

One thought is louder than the rest. If I can just get inside her, maybe everything else will make sense.

She parts her thighs and I know I can't fight it any longer.

I line myself up between her legs and thrust forward slowly, filling her in a long, deep stroke.

Maren lifts her hips, moving to set the pace she wants. It's hot as hell and I follow her lead.

With each deep stroke of my body inside of hers, I can feel it. Something's changing. *We're changing.* Growing closer. My heart aches because I want more, but also because it's the very thing I've been terrified of since this began.

"Right there," she whimpers, body shivering.

I find a deep spot within her and Maren cries out.

"Yes. Come on my cock. That's it," I groan when I feel her tighten around me. All her muscles tense at once and I have to fight back the deep moan that pours out of me.

So good.

I come then in long, hot pulses that go on forever while Maren kisses my neck and tells me how good I feel.

When it's over, I'm reluctant to withdraw, but with one last kiss to her temple, I do. I'm dizzy and spent and more satisfied than I ever recall being.

Free Bonus!

To receive a FREE ebook of *One Night with the Rebel*, a short (and HOT!) story, enter your email address at the link below and I'll send it straight you!

kendallryanbooks.com/onenightwiththerebel

Acknowledgments

A giant tackle-hug and a glass of fizzy champagne to all the readers out there for grabbing *The Boyfriend Effect*. You are the reason I get to continue bringing my stories to life, and I truly hope you loved it as much as I did. I can't wait to bring you more in this series! Up next is the story of the grumpy Wolfie Cox.

A huge amount of gratitude is owed to my lovely assistant, Alyssa; to my editors Rachel and Pam; to my agent, Jane; and my audio production team. You're all truly outstanding at what you do.

To my sweet little family . . . I couldn't do it without you. Thanks for helping me hang on to whatever little sanity I had left trying to write and homeschool during a pandemic. Wowzers—10/10 dislike. Do not recommend. But we're still smiling, right? Love you guys.